The Farmyard Mystery

David Pearson

* * *

More compelling crime stories from David Pearson:

The Galway Homicides – fifteen books set in the West of Ireland
The Dublin Homicides – six books set in Dublin

The Wexford Homicides – two books set in the "Sunny South-East" of Ireland

See them all on the website:
www.booksbypearson.com

Published by Booksbypearson ®
Dublin, Ireland

ISBN Number: 978-1-9998270-6-9

BooksByPearson

Chapter One

It was a cold and overcast night as Pat Nevin drove his Mitsubishi Outlander along the narrow lanes, heading for home. His son, Conor, sat beside him, feeling rather nervous at the speed his father was going.

"Jesus, Dad, take it easy, will ya? What's the hurry?" Conor asked.

The lights on the big 4x4 penetrated the inky blackness for a few hundred metres, but there was no other light available at 3:30 a.m. If there was a moon, it was obscured by the clouds scurrying across the sky and the dense foliage of the trees overhead, which occasionally shed more of their leaves in the strong breeze, making the road surface slick.

Pat didn't slow down.

"I've driven these roads all my life, son. I know what I'm about, so you can relax. We'll be home in a few minutes."

Conor said nothing but tightened his grip on the handle above the door.

The vehicle hurtled on, bouncing along the uneven surface of the narrow single-track road that led to the homestead where Pat, his wife Eileen, Conor and his younger brother, Shane, all lived.

Much to Conor's relief, his father finally swung the big car between the gates of their driveway and sped up to the yard at the back of their house. He brought the car to an abrupt halt, the headlights now illuminating the padlocked door of a large, metal shed – painted dark green – in front of them.

"I'll open the barn. You get the bag from the back," Pat said.

"Right."

* * *

Pat Nevin removed the keys from the ignition, making sure to leave the headlights on, opened the driver's door and got out. He started across the broken concrete apron in front of the barn, his form illuminated by the headlights.

As he walked purposefully on, a dark shape emerged from the shadows, but Pat didn't hear the approach until it was too late. As he turned, a long blade was thrust up through his torso and penetrated his heart, stopping it instantly. Pat, carried forward by his momentum, fell face down without making a sound. He was dead before he hit the ground.

* * *

Conor was busy fetching the large black holdall from the back seat of the car. His view of the area in front was obscured by the open rear door, and his sight was impaired by the brightness of the interior light, so he didn't see the fate that had befallen his father.

As he closed the door of the jeep, he thought he heard something behind him, and as he turned to see where the noise was coming from, a long blade was thrust upwards into him from his lower abdomen. His hand went to his stomach, his knees buckling as he folded onto the wet concrete.

The assailant wrestled the handles of the black bag from the young man's hand as he bled out on the ground, turned and jogged across the yard, back into the undergrowth from whence he had come.

* * *

Inside the house, Eileen Nevin, who'd been in a restless sleep listening out for her husband and son to return from whatever mission had taken them out at such an ungodly hour, sensed, more than observed, the arrival of the Mitsubishi. She threw the duvet back and got out of bed, going to the window of the upstairs bedroom and pulling aside the curtains. She looked out onto the yard. The lights of the vehicle made it difficult to process the scene easily, but she could see what she thought was the shape of someone lying on the ground in front of the barn door, and whatever it was wasn't moving. She waited anxiously, trying to figure out what was going on, and then decided she'd better go and investigate. Maybe Pat had tripped and fallen, and banged his head. But if that was the case, where was Conor?

She hastily donned her pink-and-green towelling dressing gown, shoved her feet into her slippers, turned the external light on and headed outside. Out in the yard, she spotted a shape lying on the ground in front of the jeep and ran to it, realizing it was her husband.

"Pat! Pat! What's happened? Are you OK?" Alarm had crept into her voice. She gripped her husband by the shoulder and rolled him over, revealing a pool of blood beneath his body. She could see at once that he was unresponsive. Her hand flew to her face, panic now setting in for real.

"Good God!" Eileen exclaimed then squealed, "Conor! Conor! Where are you?"

But there was no reply.

She rose unsteadily to her feet and, seeing the rear door of the Mitsubishi open, went to the side of the vehicle, fearing what she might discover. When she found her eldest son lying on the ground in a pool of his own blood, she collapsed to her knees, wailing loudly. "Oh God, God, what have you done?" she cried as the tears flowed freely down her cheeks.

* * *

Shane, the second son of the household, was awoken by the noises coming from the yard. He got up lazily, wondering what nonsense his brother and father had been up to that had resulted in such a racket. He made his way to the landing window that looked out onto the yard and peered out. He could see very little but enough to make him want to find out more, so he ran down the stairs two at a time, dressed in nothing but his pyjamas, and out the open front door.

Shane went towards the dreadful eerie sounds his mother was making and discovered her, still down on her knees, bent over his dead elder brother. By now she was almost whimpering.

"God, Mam, what's after happening?" Shane said, but his mother just muttered something incoherent and pointed. Shane, following her direction, went to the front of the car and discovered the body of his dead father.

"An ambulance, Mam. I'm going to call an ambulance. Stay with them!"

Shane ran back into the house to the kitchen where the cream telephone hung on the wall and dialled 999. The instrument rang twice before being answered by a man with a calm voice. "Emergency – which service do you need?"

"Ambulance. I need an ambulance. My father and brother have been hurt. And hurry, please, I think they're bad."

The call handler went on to elicit the Eircode for the property from Shane, and said that the ambulance would be dispatched immediately and should be there in about twenty minutes.

"What is the nature of their injuries?" the man asked.

"I don't know. There's a lot of blood, and they're both unconscious. I don't know what's happened."

The call handler then asked if Shane needed any first aid advice, and told him to keep the injured men warm and positioned on their sides in the recovery position until the ambulance arrived. He told the lad not to attempt to move them otherwise, as to do so might add to their injuries.

When the call was over, Shane grabbed a couple of woollen blankets from the house and went back outside to do as instructed, but when he got back to where his brother and mother were, she said, "It's no use, Shane.

They're gone. Both gone. My wonderful Conor and his lovely father. Both dead. What are we going to do?"

Shane placed the second blanket over his brother and kneeled beside his mother, putting his arm around her, but she couldn't be consoled. She sobbed uncontrollably.

* * *

The agent in the handling centre in Ballyshannon identified the location that Shane's plea for help had come from and, as a matter of course, notified the nearest Garda station, which in this case was Westport, in County Mayo.

Chapter Two

The assailant realized that the arrival of the Mitsubishi into the yard could have alerted someone inside the house, so he needed to get out of there – and quickly.

When he'd seen off the two men and grabbed the black holdall, he sprinted over to the wooden fence at the edge of the paved area and leaped over it in one clean jump. Once on the far side, he ran to the edge of the field he found himself in and paused to catch his breath.

He put his arms through the long handles on the black bag to fix it to his back and took off again, running along in the shade of the hedgerow until he came to the boundary of the field, which was marked by a fast-running stream about two metres wide. He slithered down the bank, using his hands on the ground to steady himself, and fell, rather than jumped, into the water. It rose almost to his knees, and he had some difficulty staying upright. But he waded across the running torrent and scrambled up the far bank, getting mud and grass all over his clothing.

Once at the other side of the stream, he paused again to catch his breath and looked back in the direction of the house, but he could see no movement of any significance. Feeling a little calmer now, he continued across the fields, stepping carefully in the darkness to avoid going into a hole and spraining his ankle. After a while, he came to the edge of the rough ground where there was a five-bar gate through which he exited, having checked carefully that there was no traffic in either direction on the road.

He crossed the road to where he'd left his motorcycle. It had been chosen for its relative silence, being a four-cylinder Honda Pan European. He mounted it, started the engine, and set off quietly down the road with his headlight still switched off.

He drove back to the Airbnb he'd rented under an assumed name on the outskirts of Castlebar, removed all of his clothing, and got into the shower. A few minutes later, he emerged and dressed in all new clothes, bundling the old ones into a bin liner for disposal. He opened the black bag that he'd taken from the jeep and looked inside. It was all there. He smiled to himself.

He sat down on the sofa, picked up his mobile phone, and dialled a number. After five rings, a voice at the other end said simply, "Yes."

"It's me. Job done."

"Have you got it?"

"Yes."

"All of it?"

"Yes, all."

"And Nevin?"

"Sorted."

"OK. Bring it to me." And the line went dead.

Chapter Three

The western region of An Garda Síochána had recently been reorganized. The counties of Mayo, Roscommon and Longford had all been brought together, and as a result, many personnel had been moved around, rather like pieces on a chessboard. Management had said this was to optimize the use of resources and provide the most effective Garda presence commensurate with the needs of the people they served. Some argued that the reality was a little different, but in the way the rank-and-file officers operated, they would make it work as soon as everyone had settled into their new roles.

It was by this means that Detective Inspector Martin O'Shea, along with Detective Sergeant Deirdre Maguire, had found themselves thrust together along with a few Detective Gardaí in the Westport station, answerable to Superintendent Derry O'Connell, who was stationed temporarily in Westport too. The Westport station was manned around the clock, but after 7 p.m., it was usual for just the sergeant in charge and a number of uniformed officers to continue to keep the peace in the area. A squad car was available to the uniformed crew, but if anything serious happened, Castlebar was usually called upon for backup.

The desk sergeant in Westport was just brewing a cup of tea when the call came in. It had been a quiet night so far, with just a few calls about a bit of boisterousness in the town after the pubs closed, but that had been seen to hours ago, and there had been no arrests. He was surprised to hear that there were two causalities at this hour of the morning in a remote location west of the town.

When he'd finished speaking with the call centre, he got on the radio to the squad car which was still out patrolling.

"Westport station to Mike Yankee 22," he said into the microphone on his desk, using the call sign for one of the officers in the patrol car.

"Go ahead Westport," came the reply.

"Morning, Tom. We've had a call from the ambulance service about two casualties out near Mucklagh. It's a farm owned by a Pat Nevin. We have no further details yet, but I think you should go out and see what's going on."

"OK, Sarge. Can you give me the map reference, and we'll head over? I think that's out beyond the golf club. It's only about ten minutes away, if I have the right place."

The sergeant called out the Eircode that the call centre had provided so the second Guard, who was a passenger in the squad car, could put it into the on-board satnav.

"Yes, Sarge, show us attending. I have it now. We'll be there in a few minutes."

* * *

The ambulance had arrived in the farmyard ahead of the Garda car, and the paramedics were attending to the two men who were still lying on the wet concrete.

The Garda car pulled in behind the ambulance, and Tom Dolan got out and walked over to where the female paramedic was examining Pat Nevin for vital signs.

"Morning, Breda," Dolan said, recognizing the woman from previous encounters.

"Morning, Tom. This is a bad do altogether, I'm afraid. It looks as if they're both deceased."

"God, are you sure?"

"We've been working on them for a few minutes now, but neither of them has a pulse, and they aren't breathing. They've both lost a lot of blood too. I'll have to pronounce them dead once I've spoken to Jimmy. He's still working on the lad."

"Any idea what caused it?" Dolan asked.

"Yes. They were both stabbed by one or more assailants. Very deep wounds, so a long blade, and whoever was wielding it knew what they were doing. They didn't stand a chance."

"Christ! Well, look, if they are both gone, you'd better leave them here till we get the pathologist out. And I'll have to call reinforcements from Westport too. Did you see any sign of a weapon?"

"No. But in fairness, I didn't really look for it. I was focused on the victims," Breda replied.

"Oh, right. OK. Well, when you're done here, put something over them, and I'll tape off the yard when you've gone till the troops arrive. I can't believe what happened here. I mean, for starters, what were they doing out and about at this time of night in any case?" Dolan said, but it was a rhetorical question.

* * *

DI Martin O'Shea was in a deep sleep. It took several minutes of persistent vibration and muted ringing for the mobile phone on the nightstand beside his marital bed to penetrate his slumber. He reached out to the glowing instrument and answered it sleepily, hoping it hadn't disturbed his wife, who, thankfully, appeared to be still asleep.

"Yes," he whispered into the phone.

"Good morning, Inspector. This is Sergeant O'Rahilly in Westport. We've had a report of two suspicious deaths at a farm out at Mucklagh. Tom Dolan is out there now, and he said it looks like the men have been stabbed. Dolan has requested a senior officer to attend."

"What the hell time is it, Sergeant?" O'Shea asked.

"Eh, 4.45 a.m. by the station clock, sir," the sergeant said, and then remained silent.

"Shit! OK. I'm on my way. Can you raise DS Maguire as well and get her out? No reason why she shouldn't have her sleep disturbed too. And you'd better call the state pathologist's office. Do you know if the media are aware?" O'Shea asked.

"I don't think so, sir. I'll text you the Eircode then and show you in attendance, shall I?"

"Yes. And let's keep the media out of it for now, OK?"

"Yes, sir. Of course."

O'Shea had been relocated to Westport from Sligo, where he'd served his time initially as a uniformed Garda and later as a detective, before working his way up through the detective sergeant rank to his current position as detective inspector. His move to Westport wasn't entirely unwelcome. His wife, Angela, was a Mayo woman and had welcomed the transfer, as it brought her nearer to her parents, who lived close by in Louisburgh. After a short search, she and her husband had found a well-appointed and relatively new detached house on the outskirts of town, and the move had been executed smoothly, thanks to Angela's very capable project management skills. The pair had settled in remarkably quickly, and O'Shea was enjoying being the senior detective in the small team allocated to Westport under the new arrangements.

Chapter Four

Detective Sergeant Deirdre Maguire was originally from Tipperary, where her parents ran a large, and successful, dairy farm. She'd served her time as a uniformed Garda in Thurles, transferring to plain clothes as a detective after three years, then moved to Castlebar when a promotion opportunity arose that saw her uplifted to detective sergeant. Although the reorganization which had repositioned her to Westport was now some time behind them, she still lived in Castlebar, where she had a smart, new, one-bedroomed apartment close to all the necessary amenities that the town had to offer. At 33, which was young for her rank, Maguire was a keen fitness addict and enjoyed working out at the local gym two or three times a week, which kept her in excellent physical condition. Standing at five foot nine, with her strength and fitness, she reckoned she could hold her own with most of the scallywags who decided from time to time to take her on.

But early mornings weren't Deirdre Maguire's strong point, so when her phone awoke her just before 5 a.m., she wasn't best pleased.

When she'd finished talking to the desk sergeant from the Westport station, she got out of bed, changed into nicely tailored blue jeans, a shirt and a warm navy zip-up fleece, and combed out her shoulder-length brown hair in the bathroom mirror.

"You'll have to do, girl," she said to her reflection – there was no time to apply any make-up – and went downstairs to her Skoda Fabia.

At that hour of the morning, there was virtually no traffic, so Maguire urged her car along at well above the 80 kph speed limit, covering the distance from Castlebar to Westport in just over ten minutes. She turned left in the town, onto Golf Course Road, and a few minutes later arrived at her destination – the Nevin farmhouse. She pulled her car in behind O'Shea's Toyota Camry and got out.

"Morning, boss," she said to O'Shea. "What's the story here then?"

"I'm still trying to figure it out, Deirdre. We have two dead. Pat Nevin and his son Conor, it seems. The ambulance crew say they were both stabbed with a long blade, and the killer knew what he or she was doing. Mrs Nevin is inside with their other son, Shane. Would you go in and have a chat with them? See if you can find out what they were doing out at this hour?"

"Sure, boss. Do we know what time it was when they were killed?" Maguire asked.

"Not exactly. But working back from the time the call came in, it was probably sometime around four o'clock. The pathologist may be able to give us a more accurate estimate when she gets here."

"Right. I'll see what the family can tell us," Maguire said and walked off towards the house, which was brightly lit.

Eileen Nevin was seated at the scrubbed wooden

kitchen table nursing a mug of tea. Shane sat beside her with his arm around her shoulders, trying to comfort her. He looked up when Maguire entered the room.

"Sorry, who are you?" Shane asked.

"I'm Detective Sergeant Deirdre Maguire. You must be Shane. I'm really sorry, Shane, Mrs Nevin. This is an awful thing to happen. I know you're probably both in shock, but would you be up to answering a few questions for me? The sooner we can get information in a situation like this, the better the chance of catching whoever did this terrible thing."

"We'll try. But don't upset my mam any more. I've put a drop of whiskey in her tea, but she's not good."

Maguire could see what the lad meant. His mother's complexion was drained, and her face was streaked with tears. Her grey hair was untidy, and she appeared to be shaking a little as she sat looking at the wall saying nothing.

Maguire walked round to the far side of the table and sat in the third of four old rail-backed chairs that matched the table. "I won't keep you long, Shane. Is there anyone you can get to come and be with you this morning? It might help your mother."

"I'll see if Mam's sister will come across. She lives out near Foxford on the edge of Lough Conn. She has a guest house, but I doubt if there's anyone staying at the minute. I'll call her in a while," Shane said.

Maguire was impressed with how together the young man appeared under the circumstances. She decided to press on with a few questions.

"Shane, do you know what your brother and your

dad were doing out at this hour of the morning?"

"No, I haven't a clue. They sometimes did go out late on in the jeep, but I don't know what they were up to."

Maguire studied the boy as he spoke, and it seemed to her that he was telling the truth. You got a sense of people's sincerity under questioning after a while in the Gardaí.

"Could they have been hunting game or something?"

"No, I don't think so. We don't have any weapons, like a shotgun or anything, here. We're just farmers," Shane said.

"What type of farming do you do?" Maguire was keen to establish a rapport with the young man and felt that some general questions about their lives would help.

"Dad raises beef cattle. He buys them at the market in spring and brings them on over the summer on the grass. Then he sells them to the factory coming into winter and just keeps a few for the following year."

"So you have some cattle on the farm now then?"

"Yes. About twenty. They're kept indoors in the barn at this time of year. I'll have to go and feed them a bit later."

"Do you ever have any trouble with the cattle or the farm machinery?" Maguire asked.

"How do you mean?"

"Well, have you ever had anything stolen or interfered with?"

"No. Nothing like that. We're well off the beaten track here. If you didn't know the place, you'd never find it."

"I'm sorry to have to ask, Shane, but do you know if your father or Conor had any enemies?"

Before Shane could reply, his mother suddenly sprang

to life.

"Pat Nevin was a good man, Sergeant. He worked hard and long to provide for us, and he went to Mass every Sunday to thank the Lord for what we have. You'd be better off out there trying to find whoever has done this wicked thing and stop asking us bloody stupid questions, casting aspersions on my family."

When she'd said her piece, she resumed staring at the wall, but a fresh torrent of tears fell from her eyes.

Shane tried to comfort her, but she was in a world of her own.

"Shane, did your dad have a computer?" Maguire asked.

"No, but Conor has a laptop for college stuff."

"What was he studying at college?"

"Agricultural science of course. He's the eldest, so he'll inherit the farm in time. Or should I say, he would have. God, this is terrible," he said, and started to cry.

Maguire sensed that there was nothing further to be gained, so she politely excused herself – leaving her business card on the table and asking Shane to contact her if anything further occurred to him – and made her way back out into the yard, reflecting on the tragedy that had so suddenly descended onto this apparently ordinary family.

Chapter Five

Back outside, Maguire caught up with O'Shea, who was standing close to the Mitsubishi jeep, keeping well clear of the two bodies that were still lying on the wet concrete.

"Anything interesting?" he asked Maguire as she approached.

"No. Nothing. They have no idea what the two men were doing out at this hour, or so they said, and I believe the young lad, at least. Not so sure about the mother, but she's in no fit state to be interrogated just now."

"OK. Well, she'll keep. Forensics are on their way, and Dr Mulhall should be here in about an hour. She's coming from Dublin by road. Listen, can you stay here and manage the scene? See if you can find their mobile phones. I want to get back to the station and start investigating Pat Nevin. And I want to put out the usual appeals on the early-morning radio shows as well. When the lab boys get here, I want them to go over the jeep thoroughly. Whatever this is about, there could well be clues in the vehicle. And see if you can get the bodies out of here as soon as possible too. Then we can have a proper go at the crime scene," O'Shea said.

His instructions had been delivered rather curtly, but Maguire wasn't bothered. The two of them had a good working relationship, and she couldn't blame him for being a bit direct at this hour of the morning.

* * *

Maguire waited patiently at the scene of the murders for various groups to arrive. First to get there were the forensic crew, or Scene of Crime Unit, as they liked to be known. The team consisted of three officers – two men and a woman – who promptly donned white paper suits on arrival and set about carrying out a detailed examination of the site.

Maguire approached the man she knew to be the team leader. "Morning, Kevin. Thanks for turning out so early. This is a bad one. Two deceased. Paramedics think they were stabbed, but we'll know more when the pathologist arrives. It's Dr Mulhall. I'm afraid she drew the short straw, but I've worked with her before. She's top-notch."

"Yes, I know the good doctor too. Not much gets past her. Look, we'd better get started. Anything in particular you want us to explore?" Kevin Walsh asked.

"Yes, please. The inspector wants you to give the jeep a really good going-over, and we need to establish how the assailant escaped. He may have just jogged off down the drive, but maybe not. See if you can find any traces. This yard is pretty open to the fields, but it's not the sort of place you'd walk to or cycle to if you wanted to kill someone and get away undetected. And obviously keep an eye out for a weapon, and we need to find the father's mobile phone too."

"I hear you. OK, we'll get on it. Are you going to hang around?" Walsh asked.

"Yes, I'll wait for the doctor. See what she says, and I'd better see the bodies off as well. I imagine they'll be going to Mayo University Hospital in Castlebar. I think they have the necessary facilities. Let me know at once if you find anything interesting."

When Walsh went off to instruct the team and get started examining the scene, Shane Nevin came out of the house and approached Maguire.

"Excuse me, Sergeant. Mam wants to know how long you'll be here," the young man said.

"Hello, Shane. How's she bearing up?"

"I gave her a drop more whiskey, and she seems a bit calmer now. So what's the story?"

"I'm waiting for the assistant state pathologist to arrive to examine your dad and brother, and our scene of crime team are working the yard now looking for clues. You really should stay indoors, Shane. There's a risk of contamination. It'll just be for a couple of hours. Tell me, do you have a vehicle yourself?"

"Not really. I mean I have a quad bike that I use to go around inspecting fences and seeing to the animals when they're out. It's in the shed there."

"Do you have keys to the shed?"

"Dad keeps them on his keyring, but I think there's a spare set inside. Do you want me to get them?"

"Yes, please."

Shane walked off back into the house, and a few minutes later, he returned holding out a small bunch of keys. "I think these are the ones that open the shed. It has three big padlocks on it for security. Do you want me to try them for you?"

"No, thanks. Just give them here. It might be best if

you stayed with your mother until we've finished."

"Oh, yes, of course. Righto."

When the lad had gone back indoors, Maguire took a pair of blue plastic overshoes from her jacket pocket and put them on. She walked over to the big green shed, which was more like a barn, and fiddled with the keys Shane had given her, finally releasing the three locks. She drew the bolt back on the shed door and pulled it towards her. The door creaked loudly as it opened, and Maguire went in, finding the light switch on the inner door frame. When she turned it on, fluorescent tubes flickered for a few moments above her before illuminating the vast interior of the place.

Inside was very neat and tidy. All along the left-hand wall there was a broad workbench, with a stout cast-iron vice bolted to the near end. Above the bench, storage was arranged in sections fixed to the wall, and lots of tins of various kinds were piled up on the shelves. The workbench itself had some mechanical bits and pieces scattered along its length, and beneath the bench, more boxes had been pushed in that looked to be overflowing with more mechanical paraphernalia.

Close to the back of the barn, Shane's dark-green quad bike sat in the centre of the floor. It was surprisingly clean, given that it was allegedly used out in the muddy fields, but perhaps Shane took great care of the vehicle as it seemed to be his only method of getting about.

Maguire didn't want to disturb the inside of the shed or its contents. There would be time enough for that when forensics had finished with the scene outside. But there could be something relevant in the place. After all,

Pat Nevin had been going to it at four in the morning, which was at least unusual.

As Maguire emerged from cover to go in search of Kevin Walsh, she observed that yellow footplates had begun to appear all over the yard, protecting the actual crime scene from contamination.

Chapter Six

It was 6:30 a.m. when the assistant state pathologist rolled into the farm in her brightly coloured Toyota Land Cruiser. She parked just short of the cordon Garda Dolan had put up and got out, pausing to don a white paper scene-of-crime suit and grab her bag, which was packed with a variety of gruesome medical implements. She walked across the yellow footplates into the yard and stopped adjacent to the jeep, where the body of Conor Nevin still lay on the concrete. The darkness was beginning to give way to the dawn, the sky having turned from pitch-black to navy blue in anticipation of the day ahead.

Maguire approached and greeted Dr Mulhall. "Morning, Doc. Meet Conor Nevin, deceased. As far as we can tell, he was stabbed during the wee small hours, and his father is just over there too – same story," Maguire said, nodding towards the second body.

"Hello, Deirdre. A bit unusual, isn't it? Two for the price of one as they say!"

Maguire was used to Mulhall's rather dark humour. She figured it was her way of dealing with the grim scenes she regularly encountered.

"Yes. We're not sure what's been going on. They're father and son, and as far as we can tell, they came back from somewhere in the 4x4 at around 4 a.m., and then this happened. But I'll ask you to confirm all of that when you've examined them."

"Right. I'd better get to it then," Mulhall said.

She placed a bright LED torch around her head to illuminate the scene clearly, kneeled on the ground and gently probed the corpse of Pat Nevin, easing back his clothing to get a good look at the wounds. Then she took out a small ruler and measured the incision in his body. All the while, her assistant – a tall, rather gaunt young man – was clicking away on his digital camera all around the body and zooming in on the examination site to capture as much pictorial information as possible.

Mulhall reached into her kitbag, took out a few cotton buds and gently swabbed the site of the wound before placing them into a long glass tube and sealing it. She looked all over the remains then, with the help of her cameraman, gently rolled Nevin onto his back and continued her observations. After ten minutes had elapsed, she finally stood up, removed the face mask she'd put on earlier and spoke to Maguire, who was still standing nearby.

"You were right of course. A single stab wound with a bladed weapon in through the back and straight into the heart, I wouldn't wonder. I'll be able to confirm that later when we get him back. Whoever did this has excellent knife skills. That's not an easy one."

"Can you tell me anything about the weapon that was used, Doc?"

"It has a blade of about three centimetres wide. Not serrated. Maybe something like a carving knife, but with a stiff blade. When you find it, it will have blood and skin residue near the hilt, even if it's been cleaned. Now, I'd better go and have a look at the son."

Mulhall and her anonymous assistant moved to where Conor was lying. He was half on his side, and his hand was still grasping his stomach where the fatal wound had been inflicted. There was much blood pooling around him on the ground, and Mulhall had to be careful not to get covered in it as she examined the corpse. After a few minutes, she stood once again and addressed Maguire.

"Much the same story here, except that he didn't die instantly. His ticker went on pumping for a few minutes, hence all the blood. Same type of wound though. I'd say it was the same weapon, but of course I can't guarantee that."

"Which of them was attacked first?" Maguire asked.

"Hmm… not sure. Isn't that your job? But if I was to guess, I'd say dad copped it first, and then the lad was done, though how he didn't see what was happening to his father is a bit of a puzzle. Oh, and he had something in his hands when he fell. There are a few black fibres still there. It looks as if it was wrenched out of his grip as he lay on the ground."

"Would the perpetrator be splattered with blood?" Maguire asked.

"Almost certainly, especially his shoes and the bottom of his trousers, and maybe his hands too."

"OK. Thanks, Doc. When do you think you'll be doing the post-mortems?" Maguire asked.

"I'll probably try to get to them later on. If you come over to the hospital at around 4 p.m., that should be about right. I'll get these two away in the ambulance now – let you have a proper go at the scene."

"OK. Thanks. See you later."

Dr Mulhall signalled to the crew standing nearby that it was time to remove the bodies, and they were placed in dark body bags and loaded up. The handlers treated the deceased with great respect and were careful not to inflict further damage on the remains.

When the small convoy had departed, Kevin Walsh came across to where Maguire was standing. "Hi, Sarge. Just to let you know, we found a mobile phone over there at the edge of the yard. Looks like it might have been kicked away into the grass. The screen is broken, but we should be able to get stuff off it anyway once we get it back to the station."

"Good work, Kevin. Anything else?"

"Not really. I think the killer may have run off across the field. The grass is a bit flattened, as if someone ran across it, but I'm afraid it doesn't lead us conveniently to a place where he parked his car. I'm thinking of getting a dog unit out to see if we can find out a bit more. Oh, and the jeep is interesting."

"Go on," Maguire said.

"Well, there are muddy footprints on the floor on both the driver's and passenger's side. We might be able to establish where the soil is from when we get it back. And there are traces of soil on the back seat too. Looks as if something that had been on the wet ground was left there at some stage recently. And, best of all, the on-board computer tells us that the last journey the car made was 37 km, so that means they were either 38 km away, or 19 km if they didn't turn off the engine at their destination. Sorry I can't be more specific, though I can say that the vehicle was using diesel at the rate of nine litres per 100 km."

"Fascinating, but the distance thing could be handy. Will you be much longer here?"

"Do you think I should get the dog out?"

"Yes, I do. We need to try and find out where chummy went after he killed these two, and how he got away. Stick with it for a while. I'm going back into town now. Can you give me the phone? I'll get it signed in at the station so we can get working on it straight away."

Walsh retrieved the phone – which by now was bagged up in a plastic evidence container – and handed it to Maguire.

"Great. See you later then."

"Cheers."

Chapter Seven

DI O'Shea had arrived at the Garda station in Westport before anyone else, save for the remnants of the night shift who were slowly departing. He'd used the time productively to set up a whiteboard in the open-plan area of the detective unit which would serve as an incident room for all those involved in the killing of Pat Nevin and his son, Conor.

As other officers began to drift in, word soon spread amongst them about the early call out to the farmyard in Mucklagh – and the reasons for it.

At 9:15 a.m., armed with yet another cup of coffee, O'Shea called the two detective Gardaí and their civilian administrative assistant together and began to give them a briefing. He explained what had taken place at the farm and pointed to the whiteboard, where he'd written up the names of the victims in black marker. He addressed the small group.

"DS Maguire is still at the scene liaising with the state pathologist and the crime scene crew to see if they can get any evidence of who might have done this. They've recovered a mobile phone, and she'll bring that with her when she comes in later. Agnes, can you get the phone to forensics? See what they can get from it – you know, recent call list, text messages, WhatsApps and so on, and see if there are any photographs of interest too."

Agnes Gallagher was an eager young detective who'd arrived during the recent reorganization.

O'Shea was interrupted by his mobile ringing. He looked at the screen. It was DS Maguire.

"Hi, Deirdre. What's up?"

"What's up is I'm bloody freezing. Forensics are searching the area now, then they're going to give the barn the once-over. The bodies have been removed, and they're getting a truck out to lift the jeep. They want it back at the station to work on it. I'm going to come back in soon. What do you reckon?"

"Yeah, that sounds about right. No point in you freezing to death out there. Has anyone found out how the assailant got away?" O'Shea asked.

"No – not yet in any case. They're waiting on a dog unit to get here. Kevin says there could be a blood trail, if they're lucky."

"OK. What about the Mrs and the young lad?"

"They've stayed indoors. Mrs Nevin's sister is coming over soon to be with them," Maguire said.

"Right. Best to leave them alone for now. They must be shattered. Come on back, and we'll get you warmed up."

"See you soon," Maguire said and finished the call.

* * *

When Maguire got back to the station, she went immediately to the small kitchenette that had been installed at the back of the open-plan area and brewed herself a hot coffee. With her hands wrapped around the blue-and-white-striped mug for heat, she made her way into O'Shea's office.

"Hi. I'm back," she said, rather unnecessarily.

"Hi. Christ, you do look frozen! What's the story?" O'Shea asked.

"Just as I said on the phone. We'll know more a bit later on when the forensic crew have finished up and we have the PM results. Any news here?"

"Not yet. Did you give the phone to Liam?"

"Yes. He'll see if he can get anything from it. The screen is cracked, but that shouldn't be the end of the world. Did I tell you that Kevin managed to interrogate the on-board computer in Pat Nevin's jeep?" Maguire asked.

"No. Anything of interest?"

"Possibly. He said the last journey that it made was 38 km, or perhaps 19 km if it wasn't turned off between the outbound and return journey."

"That is interesting."

O'Shea turned to a large shiny map of the entire area that was pinned up on the wall behind the desk. He took a red marker and drew a freehand circle all around Westport that he guessed represented 38 km, give or take. He then took a green marker and repeated the exercise for 19 km. Both circles went quite a distance out to sea to the west of the town. To the east, the green circle came close to Castlebar, whilst the red one passed through Swinford, Knock, Claremorris and Ballinrobe to the east and south.

O'Shea stood back to admire his handiwork. "Quite a bit of ground to cover, isn't it?"

"Sure is. But let's see what more the vehicle can tell us when they've had a good go at it. You never know."

"Hmm… you're right, I guess. Listen, we'd better go back out there a bit later and interview Mrs Nevin and the other son. Do you think we should bring them in?" O'Shea asked.

"I don't think so, unless you really think that's necessary. It would make it look as if one or both of them were under suspicion. But if you think it's the right thing to do, I'll go along with it naturally," Maguire said.

"You don't think the young lad could be our killer then?"

"No, I don't. Do you?"

"We need to keep an open mind, Deirdre, till we find out a bit more about what's gone on. But maybe you're right. It might be somewhat over the top. Are you OK to come out with me later then?"

"Yes, of course. Any initial thoughts?" Maguire asked.

"I don't want to jump to conclusions till we know more, but what does it look like to you? A trip in the small hours, possibly to the coast. Two brutal murders in the middle of nowhere. There could be a drugs connection, but as I say, let's not jump the gun."

"Yeah, I see what you mean. Let's see what forensics come back with. If they were dealing or distributing, there'll be traces somewhere around."

With nothing more to talk about for now, Maguire left the room with a quick, "Catch you later," just as O'Shea's mobile sprang to life. It was his wife.

"Hi, you. What's up?"

"Hi. Nothing really. I just wanted to find out why you left so early. Is everything OK?" she asked.

O'Shea went on to outline the incident out at Mucklagh.

"God, that's awful. The poor wife! Is someone looking after her and the other son?"

"Yes, her sister is coming down to stay with them. But we have to go out later and interview them, and I can check on them then. Looks like I'll be late home, Angela."

"What's new? Will you have eaten?"

"Possibly not. I'll text you when I'm on my way."

"OK. Thanks love, and mind yourself," Angela said.

O'Shea had been married for 12 years. He'd met his wife when he was a lowly Detective Garda on temporary assignment to Castlebar. He'd been injured during an arrest and taken to Castlebar hospital to be assessed and patched up, and Angela had been the nurse that had taken care of him. He'd been immediately impressed with her caring nature, not to mention her good looks, shoulder-length dark-blonde hair and neat size-eight figure. The nurse's uniform had added to the allure.

He'd asked for a date, and things had gone from there to where they now stood, with Angela and Martin having produced two children. Their son, Dermot, was eight years old and their daughter, Aoife, ten.

Angela was used to her husband's adventures, but it didn't stop her worrying when he was caught up in violent crime. And she'd seen the results of that all too often in the hospital where she still worked.

Chapter Eight

It was mid-afternoon when Kevin Walsh phoned DS Maguire with the preliminary findings from their forensic examination of the vehicle and the murder scene's surroundings.

"Hi, Deirdre. It's Kevin. I thought you might be interested to get our preliminary findings from Mucklagh."

"Hi, Kevin. Yes, please. What have you got?"

"Well, there are three parts to it for now. Firstly, the scene itself. We got the dog handler out, and he was able to follow the scent across the fence at the side of the farmyard, and on across the fields for quite a distance. But then we met a stream, and the dog lost it. Sorry. Then there's the vehicle. This is more interesting. We analysed the soil in the driver's and passenger's footwell. Some of it comes from around the farm, as you would expect, but there are traces from another location. We're still investigating that but may have something later on. No one realizes that soil is often quite particular to a locale. And there's more."

"Go on. Don't keep me in suspense."

"Remember I told you there were traces of soil on the back seat too, as if something had been on the wet ground then left there? Based on the fibres we found and the shape of the imprint on the upholstery, we think it was a bag of some kind. Quite a big bag, I'd say."

"Any traces of drugs anywhere?" Maguire asked.

"No, nothing. And we had a good go at the barn too, but no sign of any drugs in there – or anything else of interest really."

"And I presume the bag you're talking about is nowhere to be seen?"

"Correct. When the pathologist is doing the PM, we'll get the victims' clothes and give them a good going-over for drugs. There may be something in the pockets."

"Right. Well, let me know if you get anything further. We need to try and find a motive for these crimes soon, or we'll be rightly stuck."

"Yes, I know. I'll keep you posted," Walsh said.

When the call was over, Maguire went back to O'Shea's office and brought him up to date.

"Thanks, Deirdre. Where does that leave us?" O'Shea asked.

"It looks like the assailant was after the bag from the back seat of the car. But why kill them both? He could have just robbed them and made off with the bag, couldn't he?"

"Yes, you're right. So he wanted the two men dead as well as getting his hands on the bag, whatever was in it. What does that say to you?"

Maguire thought for a moment. "There must have been something very precious in the bag, and the Nevins knew what it was, and its significance, so they had to be silenced. But it doesn't look like it was drugs. There would have been some traces left behind, I imagine."

"Seems a bit far-fetched to me. I mean what could a farmer and his student son have that called for such violence?"

"Yeah, you're probably right. We're barking up the wrong tree I guess," Maguire replied.

"As I said before, let's keep an open mind. Give me a few minutes, then we'll go back out to the farm and interview the wife and Shane."

"Yes, OK, give me a shout when you're ready."

* * *

It was a fine afternoon as O'Shea and Maguire drove out past the golf course to Mucklagh. The sun was starting to sink out over the ocean; it looked like a huge red ball that had stained the wispy clouds around it a delicate shade of pink. The roads had dried up during the day, but, as was normal in Mayo, rain was forecast for later. The county benefitted – if that's what you'd call it – from a prevailing westerly wind that brought clouds across the Atlantic Ocean where they filled up with evaporated seawater. As soon as they hit the land and were pushed up into cooler air, they condensed and dumped their soggy cargo on the ground beneath.

As they pulled into the farmyard, a shiver went up Maguire's spine as she remembered the events of the early morning. A small silver Hyundai was parked on the concrete apron that hadn't been there earlier.

"How do you want to play this, boss?" she asked her colleague.

"You lead. I'll observe. Do you think we should question the two of them together, so we can see if there's any interaction? It looks like they have visitors too,"

O'Shea said.

"Let's play it by ear. The visitor is probably Mrs Nevin's sister. She said she'd be coming over."

As they exited the car, Maguire could still feel the uneasy chill she couldn't readily account for. She'd been to many scenes of crime in her time, and some a lot worse that the one they'd encountered that morning, but she just couldn't shake her instinct that there was something very sinister about the place.

* * *

O'Shea knocked firmly on the farmhouse door, which wasn't actually fully closed, but he felt the need to announce their presence.

A moment later, Shane appeared, looking pale and a little dishevelled.

"Oh, hi, Inspector," the young man said. "Have you found out who did this?"

"Good afternoon, Shane. I was wondering if DS Maguire and I could come in? We'd like to ask your mother and yourself a few questions to help us find the culprit."

Shane glanced back over his shoulder momentarily then said, "I suppose so. But Mam is very fragile. I'm not sure she's up to it."

"We'll be as gentle as we can, Shane, but it's important to get as much information as possible at this stage. The first 24 hours after such a terrible event are crucial for us."

Shane stood aside and waved the two detectives down the narrow corridor towards the kitchen, which was at the back of the property. The house was old but generally in good order. The hallway was wallpapered in a neutral, subdued, floral pattern, and the white-painted skirting boards weren't chipped or discoloured. The floor was plain flagstones, but they were well tended and in good condition with a slight shine to them. A slim mahogany table was the only furniture in the passage, but it too was polished, as was the slender electric lamp that stood upon it, illuminating the area.

In the kitchen, Eileen Nevin, still in her dressing gown, sat at the table nursing a mug of tea. She looked drawn and frail, although O'Shea sensed a determination coming from the woman which he hadn't anticipated.

Another woman, probably in her late fifties, slim, with short brown hair going grey, and dressed smartly, sat beside Eileen Nevin. When O'Shea and Maguire entered the room, she stood up and extended her hand.

"I'm Bridget Mulligan. I'm Eileen's sister," she said calmly, looking directly into Martin O'Shea's eyes.

"Good afternoon, Mrs Mulligan. I'm Detective Inspector Martin O'Shea, and this is my colleague, Detective Sergeant Deirdre Maguire. I'm very sorry for your loss," he said, shaking her hand and noting her firm grip.

"Have you caught the bugger that did this terrible thing, Inspector?"

"It's very early days, Mrs Mulligan. We need to find out a bit more about Pat and Conor, and we were hoping that Mrs Nevin would be up to answering a few questions."

Eileen Nevin, who'd been silent up till now, spoke up. "I'll answer your questions if it'll help you catch the vermin that's destroyed my family. And if you do find him, don't bother with all that arrest malarky and the courts – just shoot the fecker through the head. Even that would be too good for him."

O'Shea nodded to Maguire, who recognized the gesture.

"Shane, could we maybe have a chat in the front room while your mam is talking to the inspector?"

"Yes, I suppose so," the young man replied.

Maguire and Shane left the room, and O'Shea sat down in the vacant chair. Bridget Mulligan offered him a cup of tea, but he declined.

"Mrs Nevin, can you tell me a bit about Pat?" he asked.

"What do you want to know?"

"Well, apart from working the farm, did he have any outside interests? Was he involved in the local GAA or the golf club, for instance?"

"Inspector, you don't know much about farming, do you? Pat put every waking hour into this place. If he wasn't tending to the animals, he was fixing up fences, or buying in feed, or sorting out the machinery, or spreading muck on the land to make the grass grow. He had no time for any of that stuff you mentioned."

"Did he socialize in the town at all?"

"Sometimes. Maybe on a Saturday, if the work was done, we'd go into Westport and have a meal in the hotel. Pat would have two or three pints, and I'd drive home. I don't drink at all."

"So he hadn't any close friends hereabouts then?"

"He knew a few of the other farmers, and he'd meet them at the markets and the like. But he was content to be busy with the farm and with us. He loved his family dearly. He was a good man, Inspector." And with that, she started to sob quietly.

O'Shea gave her a few minutes before pressing on with his questions.

"I know this is difficult, Mrs Nevin, but do you know anyone at all that might have fallen out with your husband recently?"

"I do not! Pat never bothered anyone. Like I said, he was a good man."

"Have you any idea what he was doing out and about in the small hours with Conor?"

"No. And he didn't tell me what they were up to. He was quite a private person really."

"So he didn't say where he was going last night – or why?"

"No. That's what I'm saying – he didn't say a word."

"Did Conor give any clue as to what might have been taking place?" O'Shea asked.

"He never said anything either. But it isn't a crime to be outdoors at three or four in the morning, is it?" Eileen Nevin said.

"No, of course not. But it is a bit unusual. So you don't know where they'd been then?"

"I told you, Inspector, I knew nothing about it till I heard the car coming back into the yard and saw the lights. By the time I got up to look out, it was all over," she said and sobbed some more.

"Sorry to press you, Mrs Nevin, but may I ask if you saw anyone other than Pat and Conor when you looked out the window? Someone running away maybe?"

"No, I didn't. I would have told you if I had."

Bridget Mulligan interrupted the conversation. "I think Eileen has had enough for now, Inspector, don't you? This has been an awful ordeal for her. She needs to rest."

"Yes, of course. I'm sorry to have to bother you, Mrs Nevin. And thank you for talking to me."

Eileen Nevin just looked up at O'Shea and nodded.

It was time for him to leave.

Chapter Nine

In the other room, Maguire was making slightly better progress questioning Shane Nevin.

"Tell me about your brother, Shane? What was he like?"

"What's to tell. He was a hard-working student. And when he wasn't studying, he was helping out here on the farm. We both did. Dad used to have a herdsman and a farmhand, but when things got tight a few years back, he had to let them go. So these days, it's just the three of us doing all the work. It's not easy. I don't know what we'll do now."

"You said before that Conor was studying agricultural science?"

"Yes. He was clever. Always came first or second in the class in the exams. He was due to finish next summer, and he would have got a first, I'm sure of it."

"Did he ever talk to you about his college work?" Maguire asked.

"Sometimes, but to be honest, it went right over my head. He was into microbiology, I think. You might as well be talking about nuclear physics to me. I haven't a clue."

"Have you any ideas what you want to do when

you've finished school, Shane?"

He gave a little snigger. "I was thinking maybe the Guards, or the army, or maybe a fireman or something, but all that's out the window now. I'll have to help Mam with this place. See if we can keep it going somehow."

Maguire paused for a few moments before continuing. "You mentioned before that Conor had a laptop. Is it here? And did he have a phone?"

"No, he usually left the laptop in his locker in college. The internet is very poor here, and anyway, when he was at home, he was busy with the animals, or out across the fields digging ditches or mending fences. But he should have had his phone in his jeans pocket. Didn't you find it?"

"No, but it may turn up yet. Did you ever meet any of Conor's friends?"

"Oh, yeah. Every now and then I'd go into town with him if there was something on, and Conor would introduce me. They're a lively lot. We had some good times together."

"Was there anyone he was especially close to?"

"There was a girl called Maeve in his class. He went out with her a few times. I don't think it was serious, but they seemed good with each other. I like her. She's good fun. And he used to hang around with a bloke called Adam a bit. I met him once or twice. He seemed like a nice guy."

"Do you know Maeve's second name or where she lives?"

"Eh, I think her second name is Kilcoyne. She lives with her parents."

"And what about Adam – do you know his second name?"

"No, I'm afraid not."

"I'm sorry to have to ask this, but do you know anyone who would have wanted to harm your brother at all? Did he have any enemies?"

"God, no. Not that I know of anyway. He was popular and good at his work."

"OK. Thanks, Shane. I'll leave it there for now. But if you think of anything else that might be relevant, no matter how small, please give me a call. Here's my card," Maguire said, handing it over.

Maguire went outside when she'd finished talking to Shane. She made a call back to the Garda station and spoke to Liam Staunton.

"Hi, Liam. It's me. Listen, can you do something for me?"

"Sure, Sarge. What's up?"

"Well, two things really. Firstly, can you locate a student from ATU Mayo. Her name is Maeve Kilcoyne, and she's studying ag science. I think she lives with her parents, but the college should be able to give you her address. Then I'd like you to go to the college campus and get them to open Conor Nevin's locker. See if there's a laptop in there, and if so, bag it and bring it in. OK?"

"Yes, no problem, Sarge. Are you coming back in?"

"Yes. I'll be in with Inspector O'Shea in a while."

"Right. See you then."

* * *

When O'Shea and Maguire had left, Shane sat with his mother and his aunt at the table. They were, naturally, a cheerless group, but there was something different stirring in Shane's mind – anger.

"That lot are fucking useless, mam. Did ye see the state of them. They haven't a clue. Wait till you see. They'll faff about for a few weeks to keep us happy, and then it'll get filed away under unsolved murders, and we'll never hear from them again. But I'm not having it. Don't worry, Mam. I'm going to find out who did this, and God help him when I catch up with him. That's all I'm saying."

His mother glanced up at him, looking a little bit happier than she had been previously. "You're a good boy, Shane. I think you'll do better than the Gardaí, that's for sure. But what are we going to do with the cattle?"

"I'll go across to Séan Lynch tomorrow and ask him if he'll take them. They're nearly ready for the factory in any case, and we'll get a good few bob when they're sold. Did Dad have any life insurance, Mam?"

"God, I'm not sure. I think so. All his papers are in the cupboard in our bedroom. You can have a look through them and see what you can find. I'm not up to it."

"No, don't worry yourself. I'll sort all that out."

Shane then turned to his aunt, who'd been sitting silently by, keeping an eye on her sister. "Can you stay on a bit, Aunt Bridget? Just till we can get a few things sorted out."

"Yes, of course. Don't worry – I'll stay as long as you need me."

"Thanks. I'd better go and feed the animals now. I'll be back in about an hour."

"OK, Shane," his aunt replied. "I'll have the dinner ready."

"Thanks."

As Shane worked on in the barn, he looked at the cattle that his father had enjoyed minding. They were content, chewing on the rich, pungent sileage that he forked across to put within their reach, but Shane was miserable. In the wink of an eye, his life had been turned upside down by some anonymous gouger who probably knew nothing of either of his victims. Shane's anger overwhelmed his misery.

"I'll get that bastard yet. And when I do, he'll be sorry he was ever born!" he said to himself, stabbing his fork into another lump of rotten grass.

Chapter Ten

It was late in the afternoon when O'Shea and Maguire had finished with their interviews out at the Nevins' farm. The sun was sinking below the horizon, so it would be dark soon enough.

"I don't think we'll go back to the station. I've had enough of this for today. Can I drop you home?" O'Shea asked his colleague.

"No, thanks. It would be better if you left me at the station. My car's there, and I might go in for a few minutes. I'd like to see how the others got on."

"OK. Whatever. But I'm exhausted. I'm going to head home."

By the time they got back to the Garda station, Maguire had decided to follow her boss's lead and go back to her own place in Castlebar, despite what she'd told Liam earlier. She too was tired from the day's activity, but she was feeling the restlessness that always came from the beginning of a new case.

When she got into her own car, she called a contact from her phone using the hands-free facility as she manoeuvred out of the car park and departed for Castlebar.

"Hi, Eoin, it's me," she said when the call was answered.

"Oh, hi, you. What's the craic?"

Eoin was what would be called in today's terms a friend with benefits. She wasn't going out with him seriously, and there was no commitment involved, but they enjoyed each other's company when it suited them both, and as they were both unattached, it made sense.

"I was wondering if you're free tonight? I've had a bitch of a day, and I need some light-hearted company to take my mind off things."

"I'm not sure if that's a compliment, but it sounds like a plan," Eoin said. "Where are you?"

"I'm just driving back from Westport. I'll be home in twenty minutes or so. Give me time to shower and change, then we can go out somewhere to eat. Sound OK?"

"Yeah, that works for me. I'll call for you at about eight."

"Great. Thanks. See you later."

Eoin McNally was in his thirties and worked for an international insurance company that had set up in the area. His role was to investigate large claims, so in a way, he was a kind of detective too. He had a good success rate in discovering when things weren't right with a claim, and he was highly regarded by the company.

Maguire had encountered him when she was investigating a theft a couple of years previously, and had been immediately drawn to his handsome looks and gentle demeanour. Once the case had been resolved, they'd gone out on a few dates and formed a bond with each other. The arrangement appeared to suit both of them, though Maguire wondered if it would ever develop into anything a little more serious, which she would have liked.

Eoin arrived at ten minutes past the appointed hour to find Maguire looking radiant in designer jeans and an expensive silk blouse with a cashmere cardigan over it.

"Wow. You look fabulous, Deirdre. I'm a lucky guy. Are you ready?"

"Yes, sir! More than ready. Where are we off to?" she asked, closing the door of her apartment and locking it behind her.

"Do you fancy that place down on Tucker Street? I think you can get all sorts there, and it has good reviews."

"Sounds great. I'm starving. I didn't manage any lunch what with everything going on," Maguire said.

"Great. Let's go then!" Eoin replied.

They travelled the short distance to Tucker Street in Eoin's black Audi, and when they arrived at the restaurant, they were shown to a table in a quiet spot, well away from the doors to the kitchen.

When they were seated, Eoin asked, "What would you like to drink, Deirdre?" The waitress was hovering.

"Just a small glass of white wine please. If I have any more, it'll go straight to my knees!" She smiled at the young woman.

"And I'll have an alcohol-free beer please. I wouldn't want to get arrested for drink-driving," Eoin said, looking at Maguire and smiling.

When they'd settled in, the drinks had been served and the waitress had taken their order, Eoin broached the subject of the day's events that had kept Maguire so busy.

"I heard about that thing out beyond the golf course. Is that what you've been doing?"

"Yes. I was woken from my beauty sleep at 5 a.m. if you don't mind. But it was horrible. Two dead in the most gruesome way you can imagine, and of course the family are in bits."

"Have you any idea who was behind it?"

"No, and even if I had, I couldn't say. But it was a very tidy assassination. No amateur, that's for sure."

"Should we be worried that there's a madman on the loose?"

"No, I don't think so. These two were definitely targeted, but we have no idea why yet."

Just then, the waitress arrived with two plates of delicious-looking food.

"Thanks," Maguire said. "That looks fantastic."

They ate their food, which was indeed sumptuous, more or less in silence, and when they'd finished and their clean plates had been taken away, they sat, replete, in front of two steaming cups of coffee.

"Are we going back to yours?" Eoin enquired.

"If you like. But I won't be much use to you tonight. I'm shattered."

Eoin reached across and put his hand on hers. "That's fine. It would just be nice to be in your company. But if you'd rather not..."

"Thanks. That's sweet of you."

Eoin called for the bill.

Chapter Eleven

Things were getting busy the following morning when Maguire arrived at the station. O'Shea was already at his desk, and out in the open-plan area, Liam Staunton and Agnes Gallagher were hunched over their computers, tapping away.

When O'Shea saw his sergeant arriving, he called her into his office.

"Hi, Deirdre. I'd like to work out a plan for the day with you. Superintendent O'Connell has already been bending my ear asking how the investigation's going. He's getting heat from the press office."

Superintendent Derry O'Connell was originally from Limerick but had served his time in a number of different locations around the country before ending up in Mayo. He was a big man with short grey hair, a round, ruddy face and a presence you could feel as soon as he entered a room. He'd been located temporarily in Westport to oversee the latest reorganization – a task that wasn't really enough to keep him fully occupied – so he was inclined to look over O'Shea's shoulder rather more than was comfortable for the DI.

"Blooming hell. Give us a chance, boss," Maguire said.

"Yes, I know, but we need to be seen to be focused at least, even if we haven't a clue. Did anyone locate Conor's girlfriend?"

"I'll check that now, boss. What do you want to do then?"

"I'd like to talk to the girl. She may have some good information about his associations and his activities away from the farm. And we need to do some serious digging on Pat Nevin too. So far, we don't even know which of them was the target. Was it Pat or Conor? Do you know if anyone collected Conor's laptop from the college?"

"No, sir, I've only just arrived. But give me half an hour and I'll find out about everything."

"OK, thanks, Deirdre."

Maguire went outside and spoke to Staunton. "Liam, did anyone see Conor's girlfriend yesterday, do you know?"

"Yes, Sarge. Uniform called out to ATU to tell her the bad news. I spoke to the Garda afterwards. She said the girl was pretty cut up. Hardly surprising, I suppose," Staunton said.

"Did this officer get anything out of her?"

"No. She was in bits apparently. The female officer had to drive her home."

"OK. Well at least we have an address then. Any news on Conor's laptop?"

"Oh, yeah. The college refused to open his locker. They said we needed a warrant. They were pretty awkward. More concerned about how the killings would affect the college's reputation it seems," Staunton said.

"We'll see about that. I think the DI and I are going out there shortly. O'Shea will sort it. In the meantime, can you get digging on Pat Nevin? All the usual stuff – known associates, phone records, any previous interaction with us, finances and so on."

"Right, Sarge. I'll get to it straight away."

Maguire went back in and brought O'Shea up to date.

"OK. Let's go. University first, then Maeve Kilcoyne's place."

* * *

They drove along the N5 past Upper Drummindoo and on to Cloggernagh East before turning onto the R309 near Dernagro. The day was cool but quite bright, if not exactly sunny. The roads were dry, and they made good time, arriving at the ATU campus just 20 minutes after leaving Westport.

The ATU Castlebar campus was originally built as a hospital in 1866 and was used for some time as a lunatic asylum, before becoming St Mary's Hospital early in the twentieth century. The buildings were rather grey in appearance and still looked somewhat institutionally dour, but inside, things were different. Since the college opened in 1994, the venue had been seriously overhauled and now provided modern facilities for over 1,000 students studying a wide range of subjects.

O'Shea and Maguire got out of their car and walked towards the entrance.

"Looks a bit grim to me," Maguire said.

"Not exactly an architectural gem, I agree. But I imagine it's a pretty good place to study if you're from these parts. Saves you having to travel to Galway or Sligo," O'Shea replied.

"Yes, I suppose."

Once inside, they approached the reception desk, which was manned by a thin man in a drab, well-worn grey suit that hung loosely from his emaciated frame. His pallor was almost the same colour as the suit.

"How can I help you?" he asked.

O'Shea held up his identification card. "I'm DI O'Shea, and this is my colleague, DS Maguire. We need access to Conor Nevin's locker please."

"Do you have a warrant?" the man asked rather sourly.

Maguire could sense O'Shea stiffening beside her. He leaned forward until his face was level with the man behind the desk. He spoke slowly and deliberately.

"Now look here. Conor Nevin and his father were sliced open in the small hours of yesterday at their farm out at Mucklagh. Conor bled to death on the cold wet concrete, just along from his father's dead body. I want to catch their killer. I believe there may be something that would help me to do that stored in Conor's locker. So if I have to go back to Westport and get my superintendent to issue a warrant to give me access to it, then I will. But I might also arrest you for obstructing the Gardaí in the execution of their duty, and I don't think you'd fare too well in prison, do you?"

The man held O'Shea's stare for a few moments, presumably processing what had been said to him. Then he reached into his desk drawer, grabbed a large bunch of small keys, stood up and walked away down the corridor without saying a word.

The three of them traversed a series of long corridors with tiled floors and glossy cream paint on the walls. Here and there were noticeboards with posters of various kinds pinned to them. Eventually, they came to a room with a pale-green door leading to a large, dimly lit area storing what looked like hundreds of lockers. The single window at the end of the space was grimy and afforded little light.

The man in the grey suit slipped down between two towers of lockers and stopped. He sorted through the big bunch of keys till he found the right one, opened a locker door and stood back.

"Thank you. That wasn't so hard now, was it?"

The man said nothing. He just slinked away silently.

"Right. Give me a nice big evidence bag, Deirdre. There's quite a bit in here." He started with a sleek silver-grey laptop, dropping it into the bag Maguire was holding open. He asked for another evidence bag and filled it with four plastic folders containing documents. Finally, he placed a tracksuit top in yet another bag.

"OK, we need to get this lot back to the station. Can you call a car from the local nick to take it back and phone Agnes to make sure she gets it from them?"

"Sure. What are you going to do?" Maguire asked.

"I'm going back in to have another word with Prince Charming. I want to see if Conor had any more stuff anywhere on campus. See you in a few minutes, then we'll go looking for Maeve Kilcoyne."

Maguire was glad to get back outside into the fresh air. As she waited for her colleague, her mind turned to the history of the place they were in.

"If buildings could talk, I'd say this one could tell a tale or two," she said to herself and shivered – not from the cold but from the thoughts of what might have gone on there in the past.

Chapter Twelve

Maeve Kilcoyne lived in a modest family home on the outskirts of Castlebar with her parents and two younger sisters. As O'Shea's satnav guided them faithfully to the address, they observed that the houses had at one time been local authority owned but presumably had been sold off to the tenants some years ago. Several of the properties on the Kilcoynes' road had been extended and improved, although number 38, where Maeve lived, looked more or less original, with a pebble-dashed façade and old iron single-glazed windows. Its saving grace, if there was one, was that it was at the end of a terrace of six houses, which meant that there was room at the side to park a vehicle off the street and store the rubbish bins out of sight. More industrious occupants might have extended the property into this space, but that hadn't happened here.

O'Shea parked his car half up on the footpath to avoid obstructing through traffic on the narrow thoroughfare, and the two of them got out. They walked up the short path to the front door, past a tiny patch of grass, bordered by a narrow flower bed which had three rose bushes still with a few rather tired-looking pink blooms. He knocked on the front door.

After a few moments, a woman who looked to be in her late forties opened the door. She was quite small in stature, but had a slim figure and a pretty face, with high cheekbones and sparkling blue eyes. Her short blonde hair was well cared for and nicely styled. She was wearing skinny denim jeans and leather calf-length boots, with a warm woollen pullover.

"Hello. Mrs Kilcoyne?" O'Shea asked.

"Yes. Who are you?"

"I'm Detective Inspector Martin O'Shea from Westport Garda, and this is my sergeant, Deirdre Maguire. We're looking to speak with Maeve Kilcoyne. Is she here?"

The woman seemed a little flustered by the enquiry but recovered quickly, saying, "You'd better come in. I'm sorry, the place isn't very tidy. I've been looking after Maeve. She's had a terrible shock." She stood aside and ushered the detectives into a small but very well-presented front room which had clearly been decorated in the recent past. She gestured for them to sit on the pale sofa.

"I'll go and get Maeve," Mrs Kilcoyne said and left the room.

They could hear her climbing the stairs and some muffled conversation above. O'Shea just looked at Maguire and raised his eyebrows but said nothing.

Maeve Kilcoyne entered the room with her mother behind her. The girl had inherited her mother's good looks, although she was taller, and had long, dark-brown hair flowing down over the shoulders of her pink dressing gown. She had pink slippers on her feet.

O'Shea stood up. "Thanks for agreeing to see us, Maeve. I know this is a very difficult time for you. Please sit down."

Maeve sat down rather shakily in another chair. It was clear that she'd been crying, and she looked pale and drawn, as if she hadn't slept well the previous night.

O'Shea looked across at Maguire, who got the message.

"Maeve, we're very sorry about Conor. It's dreadful what's happened to him and his father. We are investigating, and I'm sorry, but we need to ask you some questions, if you're up to it."

Maeve nodded almost imperceptibly.

Maguire paused for a few seconds before continuing. "May I ask how close you and Conor were?"

"Not really close. Like, not really girlfriend and boyfriend. But we went out a few times together, and we sort of mixed in the same groups at uni. He was great fun," Maeve said.

"Were you on the same course?" Maguire asked.

"Yes, agricultural science. But he's a lot cleverer than I am. He was into all sorts of advanced stuff that I couldn't understand."

"What sort of stuff?"

"I don't know too much about it. But he was interested in bacteria and things in the dairy industry. He was always getting samples and analysing them."

"What sort of samples?"

"I don't know. But you could ask his tutor."

"Yes, thanks, that's a good idea. And what about his friends? Who was he close to, apart from yourself?" Maguire asked.

"There's a guy called Adam Wallace that he hung around with a lot. Apart from that, he was just in the crowd. He was very popular."

"Is Adam doing ag science too?"

"God, no! He does computer science. He wouldn't know one end of a cow from the other. He's from Galway," she added, as if that would explain the lad's lack of knowledge of bovine physiology.

"I know this is hard, Maeve, but do you know anyone that might have wanted to hurt Conor?" Maguire asked.

"No, of course not! He was a lovely guy. It must have been his father that the killer was after and Conor was just in the wrong place at the wrong time. I don't know," Maeve said. She started sobbing, and her mother handed her a tissue.

"I'm sorry," O'Shea said. "Is there anything else at all you can tell us that might help us with this dreadful case?"

Maeve just shook her head.

Maguire looked at O'Shea and nodded towards the door. He read the signal.

"Right, well, thanks very much, Maeve," Maguire said, standing up and handing over her card. "We're very sorry to have bothered you. We'll leave it at that for now, but we may need to speak to you again, if that's OK?"

Maeve just nodded and looked down at the floor.

* * *

When they were back in the car, putting on their seat belts, O'Shea said to his colleague, "Well, Sergeant, what do you think?"

"I think we'd better have a very close look at Pat Nevin. C'mon. Let's get back to the ranch. The PM results should be in by now. Maybe that will tell us something."

When they got back to the Garda station, O'Shea went to his office, and Maguire went to speak to her colleagues. There was no sign of Agnes Gallagher, but Liam Staunton was at his desk, reading a file.

"Hi, Liam. Anything to report?" Maguire asked.

"Hi, Sarge. Yes. The PM on the two men is in. No surprises, I'm afraid. As we already knew, they died of stab wounds, or should I say a single stab wound each. But there is something. They found a small bag of cannabis in Conor's jeans pocket. Probably only about €20 worth, but it might be something."

"Hmm. I don't think that's anything to get worked up about. Anything more from Kevin?"

"No, they're still investigating the soil that came from beyond the farm, so we still don't know where the two of them were off to in the middle of the night."

"Damn. Just our luck. We have no idea what the motive for this was. And as for the perp, your guess is as good as mine."

"Nothing new from the mammy or the younger brother of interest then?"

"No. 'Fraid not."

Just then, Maguire's phone began to ring. She answered it and was surprised to find Mrs Kilcoyne on the other end.

"Is that Sergeant Maguire? This is Mrs Kilcoyne, Maeve's mother," the woman said.

"Yes, that's right. Hello Mrs, Kilcoyne. How can I help you?"

"Maeve has gone back to bed. She's very upset. But after you left, we were chatting over a cup of tea, and she said something. It's probably nothing, but I thought you should know."

"Yes, thank you. What did she tell you?"

"She said that Conor had been having a spot of bother with another student at the college. This other bloke – James, she called him – was keen on Maeve, it seems. And when Conor started taking an interest in her, this James fella got aggressive. He threatened Conor. Conor kind of laughed it off, but Maeve doesn't like James. She says he's a nasty bit of stuff."

"Do you happen to know James's surname, Mrs Kilcoyne?"

"Just a minute. Yes, he's James McGinty. I think Maeve said he was from Sligo but is attending Westport. Do you think he might have had anything to do with what happened?"

"Oh, I don't know. Better not to jump to any conclusions till we investigate further. But may I ask why Maeve didn't tell us this when we were at your house?"

Mrs Kilcoyne thought for a moment before replying. "Maeve is a sensitive girl, Sergeant. She would hate to cause anyone any bother. But I thought it best to tell you. She doesn't know I'm speaking to you."

"OK. I understand. Thanks for the information, Mrs Kilcoyne. We'll look into it."

Chapter Thirteen

Later that afternoon, O'Shea brought the team together for a briefing. He'd been through a meeting with Superintendent O'Connell who was, to say the least, unhappy about their apparent total lack of progress. O'Connell was getting heat from all sides – including his paymasters in Castlebar and his own press office, who were struggling to keep the media at bay – and he'd told O'Shea in no uncertain terms that progress of a positive kind was needed urgently.

"OK, folks, settle down. Now, let's see if we have anything new to bring to bear on the case. Agnes – you've been busy. What have you got for us?"

O'Shea was referring to the fact that the young detective Garda had been missing for much of the day, and he wanted to find out if she'd been usefully employed.

"Well, sir, as you know, I took delivery of Conor Nevin's laptop earlier when you recovered it from his locker at the college."

"And?" O'Shea said rather impatiently.

"And nothing, sir. Not a thing. Four emails in his inbox to do with changes to the college timetable, and one from a bloke called Adam Wallace about a party Conor had missed. No files of any significance in his sent mail either, and although there are a few Word documents, they're mostly college assignments going back over the year," Gallagher said.

Maguire stepped in. "What about his web browsing history? Anything interesting there?"

"Cleared, Sarge. Nothing. He either deleted it all, or he was using an incognito browser, like Brave or DuckDuckGo."

"That's a bit odd, don't you think, Agnes? What about his socials?" Maguire asked.

"He has a Facebook account, but I haven't been able to get into it yet. I've had a look at him through my own account, but there's not much there. Just a few friends."

"OK, well can you print off a list of his friends for me? Thanks."

"Yes, sure, Sarge."

"There is one thing new," Maguire went on. "I had a call from his girlfriend's mother. Seems he was in some kind of tug of love with another bloke over Maeve. James McGinty by name. Can we see if we have anything on him?"

Staunton volunteered for that task. "I'll check him out."

"Anything more on the father, anyone?" O'Shea asked.

No one said anything.

"Aw, come on, folks. We need to make some serious progress on this thing. I've had the super giving me an earbashing already today, and I don't want a repeat performance. Let's get busy on this."

O'Shea concluded the meeting and went back into his own office feeling frustrated.

* * *

Maguire stayed in the open-plan area, intent on giving the team a bit of a pep talk after O'Shea's outburst. She walked over to where Agnes Gallagher was seated at her desk.

"That was good work with the laptop, Agnes. But don't you think it's a bit odd that there was so little on it?" Maguire asked.

"Yes, I do. I remember when I was a student, my laptop was full of all sorts of stuff. Music, video clips, hundreds if not thousands of emails, and more besides. Anyway, at least we have it. I might as well send it to tech to see if they can recover any deleted stuff from the hard drive. Sometimes they can."

"Yes, OK, that sounds like a good plan. But leave it till tomorrow. We've all had enough for today. I'm going home now, and you should too," Maguire said.

As Maguire got her jacket and handbag, and prepared to leave the office, O'Shea came out of his den.

"Good idea, Deirdre. Fancy a quick drink?" he asked.

"No, thanks, boss. I have more ironing than you'd think possible queuing up for me at home. I'll get you again."

O'Shea smiled. "Fair enough. See you tomorrow then. We'll have a planning session at nine, OK?"

"Yes, fine. See ya."

* * *

O'Shea wasn't a heavy drinker. He occasionally went for a pint after work, usually with some colleagues, but today, he felt he needed some thinking time, and what better place to try figuring things out than in front of a nice cold pint of Guinness beside the fire in Joyce's pub, just down the street from the Garda station?

When he got to the place, he went to the bar to order his drink.

Eamon, the barman, knew O'Shea and greeted him warmly. "Ah, there you are, Martin. The usual, is it?"

"Hi, Eamon. Yes, please. Not a bad evening."

"No, although I hear there's rain on the way," Eamon replied, taking a clean pint glass and holding it at an angle under the Guinness tap.

There was a ritual to pouring a pint of Guinness so that it finished up with about two centimetres of creamy head. You filled the glass about two-thirds full, making sure that the liquid went down the side, then left it to settle until the body of the drink had gone completely black. Then it was topped off and left to settle for another couple of minutes before the finished article was presented to the thirsty customer. This gave adequate time for some chat while the process took place.

"No surprise there," O'Shea said.

"That was a terrible thing that happened with the Nevins out at Mucklagh. I suppose you're up to your neck in it?" Eamon asked.

"Yes, a nasty business. I feel very sorry for the wife and the young son. I don't know how they'll manage now."

"Yes, 'tis dreadful all right. Everyone is horrified by what happened. The Nevins are such a nice family – and well thought of in these parts."

Eamon turned his attention back to O'Shea's pint, which had settled nicely, and completed pouring, leaving the drink to finish off in front of the detective.

"Of course, there is one man that won't mourn the

passing of Pat Nevin," Eamon said, looking directly into Martin O'Shea's eyes.

"Oh. Who's that then?"

"Yer man Boggan. He lives on the other side of the lane that runs up behind the golf course and on past the back of the Nevins' farm."

"What's the story there, Eamon?"

"He's been in dispute with the Nevins for years over a field that seems to have no clear title. Boggan claims it's his. He says his father bought it from Nevin's father years ago when times were hard, but there doesn't seem to be any paperwork. The two of them were always arguing about it, and once, not too long ago, they were both in here after the market, and it got a bit physical. I had to ask Boggan to leave. He has a fierce temper on him that fella. Must be his red hair that does it."

"I see. That's interesting. And what does Boggan want with the land?" O'Shea asked.

"Ah, you know what folks round here are like about land ownership. Anyway, he has notions of building a house on it and selling it. It's the only field that has decent road frontage on his farm. It's ironic really, 'cos when they were arguing, Pat said to Boggan 'over my dead body'."

Another customer approached the bar, and Eamon went off to serve him, leaving O'Shea to ponder what had been said.

Chapter Fourteen

O'Shea brought the team together the following morning to plan the day's activities and update them on his conversation in the pub the previous evening.

"It seems that there was some aggravation between Pat Nevin and a man called Boggan over a plot of land. We need to look into that. I'm still uneasy about the fact the killer appears to have been able to get away so easily. There's no sign of a vehicle having been parked on the road outside the farm, so if the killer was able to get wherever he was going on foot, then a near neighbour would obviously fit the bill nicely."

"So you think this Boggan character might be our man?" Maguire asked.

"It's too soon to speculate, but we need to look at it closely in any case. Any luck identifying what could have been in the bag on the back seat of the car?" O'Shea asked.

"No, boss, except that it doesn't look like it was drugs. It would have left some traces on the seat, and there weren't any," Maguire said.

"What about the phone we recovered?" O'Shea asked.

Agnes Gallagher responded. "It looks to have been Conor's, but there isn't much on it. Forensics are trying to get access to any backups there might be, but it's a slow process."

"Right. Well, we need to talk to this bloke that Conor is supposed to have pissed off over his girlfriend. James McGinty. Agnes, can you track him down and go and see him? Take a uniformed officer with you, and don't take any crap from him. If he acts up, bring him in under caution," O'Shea said.

"Right, boss."

"Sir," Staunton said, "we haven't been able to recover the weapon at all. I wonder if we should spend some more time out at the site. If I'd just stabbed two men to death, I'd be very keen to get rid as soon as possible."

"You have a point, Liam. But we haven't got unlimited resources, and the area is very big. It could take days to give it a really good search. I'd prefer if we could concentrate on the people aspect of the case for a day or two and try to shake out some kind of motive. I still can't figure out the 'why' of this case at all."

"I think the wife and son hold the key to that, boss," Maguire said. "I'm not sure they've told us all that they know."

"I presume we've appointed an FLO?" O'Shea asked.

"We tried but there was no one available until tomorrow. There's a female officer coming free, and we'll brief her later and send her out there. I'll make sure she's aware that we still need information, and without compromising her role, I'll see what she can get," Maguire said.

"OK. Plans then. Agnes, can you see if there's anyone free to work on the technical stuff before you go looking for McGinty. Get them to follow up on anything recently deleted from Conor's laptop and ask them to keep going with the phone. Deirdre, can you deal with Adam?"

"Yes, boss. Can I take Liam with me?"

"Good idea. I'm going to update the super. Then I want to follow up on this Boggan bloke. Let's all keep in touch if anything breaks."

They all nodded agreement, and then the meeting broke up.

When O'Shea got back to his own office, there was a message that the desk sergeant had been looking for him.

He called the officer on the phone. "Yes, Danny. You were looking for me."

"Oh, yes, sir. I've had a call from the secretary of the golf club. He'd like you to call him. I have his number here."

Danny reeled off the number, which was a mobile phone, and O'Shea wrote it down on a yellow Post-it note.

O'Shea felt that the golf club could wait. It was probably some petty theft or other that they wanted to report, and he had bigger fish to fry. He decided to get the meeting with Superintendent O'Connell over with before calling back.

* * *

Maguire and Staunton travelled to the ATU Westport campus in Maguire's car. Staunton was in his late twenties and had only been promoted to detective earlier that year. He was tall, with curly light-brown hair and a swarthy complexion – a trait some said had been inherited from men from the Spanish Armada that had been wrecked off the west coast of Ireland in violent storms in the late sixteenth century trying to return home via the North Atlantic. Several Spanish sailors had come ashore, although a lot drowned, and those that were spared had integrated with the local community and passed on their genes.

When they were underway, Maguire asked her companion, “Is this the first murder case you’ve been involved with, Liam?”

“Yes, it is. It’s a pretty gruesome one too. What about you, Sarge – have you dealt with many?”

“I’ve been on a few all right, but not here in Westport. There was a nasty one a couple of years back in Castlebar. A man shot his wife with a 12 bore and then tried to kill himself, or so it seemed. But he was unsuccessful, and he survived to stand trial. It was fairly open and shut though. He tried to plead diminished responsibility, but that didn’t work. He got life in the end. I was first on the scene. It was horrible.”

“How do you think this one is going?”

“Not great, to be honest, Liam. If we can’t find a motive, we’ll have a tough time cracking it.”

“Do you think this Boggan character might have had something to do with it?”

“I don’t know. There’s a lot of emotion that goes on where land is concerned. But to kill two people in cold blood, that seems a bit excessive to me.”

“Yes, but I can understand if the father was killed first, the murderer would have wanted to take the son out too as he was a witness and could probably identify the perpetrator.”

Maguire nodded. “I see what you mean. But for my money, this looks to have been planned. It looks more like an assassination than a brawl over land. The killer must have been waiting for them to return from wherever they'd gone, which is also part of the puzzle. What were they doing out at that hour of the night anyway? And where did they go? And then there's the missing bag. Maybe that's what it's all about, or maybe that was just opportunistic. Who knows? We'll just need to see if forensics come back with any more on the soil. If we knew where they went, it might help us to understand a bit more about what was going on."

They arrived at the campus and found the grey man Maguire had met previously sitting at the reception desk.

"Hello again," she said. "We're looking to see an Adam Wallace. He studies computers, I think."

The man looked up at Maguire. She thought he looked even more sickly than the last time they'd met. His face was gaunt and his pallor somewhere between white and grey, and his eyes were bloodshot.

"Second floor. Turn left at the top of the stairs, down along the corridor, room B204. He should be in there."

They climbed the stairs to the second floor. The college seemed remarkably quiet, given the number of students that were studying there, but perhaps that was due to the time of day.

Room B204 wasn't just one room. It had clearly been several rooms at some time in the past, which had then been combined to create a computer laboratory. The original divisions could be seen at ceiling height, where steel joists had been inserted to support the structure when the dividing walls had been removed.

The facility had a long bench down each wall and an island in the centre. The benches and the island accommodated rows of black PCs, and in each corner, a stack of servers and communications devices blinked and hummed. There were something like 25 students all glaring intensely at their individual screens, transfixed by the images and saying nothing.

Staunton took the lead and said in a loud voice, "Adam Wallace."

Several of the students looked up at this somewhat uncouth interruption, but only one raised his hand. Staunton and Maguire walked towards the lad, warrant cards at the ready.

"Are you Adam Wallace?" Staunton asked.

The man who looked to be in his early twenties had a mop of curly brown hair and a fresh, round face. He was around six feet tall and slim. He was dressed in a black T-shirt and black jeans, with good white trainers on his feet.

"Yes, that's me. How can I help?" he asked, smiling a little cautiously.

"We'd like to have a word in private, if that's OK," Maguire said.

"Yes, sure. Let's go outside," Wallace said.

Before leaving his workstation, he logged off, and Maguire noticed that his account was password protected.

The three of them walked back along the seemingly endless corridor and down the stairs. Outside, it was cool and breezy, but there was no rain, and the clouds were high in the morning sky. As they crossed in front of the building, a grey squirrel scampered past them, onto the grass and up a beech tree that still had some amber foliage clinging to it.

"Adam, I believe you were friendly with Conor

Nevin?" Maguire began.

"God, yes. What an awful business. Have you got anyone for it yet?"

"Our investigation is ongoing, but what I wanted to ask you was what was Conor working on here at college?"

"Well, as you probably already know, he was studying agricultural science. But Conor had gone off on a bit of a tangent. He was big into bacteria and especially bacteria in dairy cows. He was going to do his final-year project on it. It was all above my head to be honest. I'm more of a techy person."

"Would he have accumulated a lot of data, do you think?" Staunton asked.

"Shit loads— eh, sorry, yes, buckets of the stuff. It was all about data really. I helped him set up all sorts of analysis using SPSS."

"SPSS?" Maguire asked.

"Yes. It's a software suite from IBM that allows you to slice and dice big quantities of data to identify patterns and averages and other features. It's a bit tricky to use, but I'm quite good with it, so I helped Conor out."

Maguire decided it was time to take a chance. "Look, Adam, we've recovered Conor's laptop from his locker here and had a good look at it. But there's no sign of any big blocks of data on it – or anything else much really. Have you any idea why that would be?"

"Yes, I would as it happens. Recently, Conor had started backing up all his data to a plug-in hard drive. He got it from China on eBay. It had massive capacity. Two terabytes if I remember correctly. He copied it all over every evening when he'd finished manipulating the data and took it away with him. Then he deleted the information from the laptop and ran a clean-up program. It was all a bit 007 if you ask me, but he said he couldn't allow what he was doing to fall into the wrong hands," Wallace said.

"Do you know what the data was about?" Staunton asked.

"Haven't a clue. I wasn't interested in the content, just the algorithms we used to analyse it all."

"OK. Thanks, Adam. That's been helpful. Oh, just one more thing. Do you know a bloke by the name of James McGinty? I think he's a student too," Maguire said.

"I've never met him, and I don't think I'd like to. Conor said he'd been bothering him. Something to do with Maeve, I think. McGinty was threatening to come and sort Conor out if he didn't lay off the girl, which was stupid really, 'cos Maeve had no time for McGinty. But it got a bit heavy, Conor said."

"Thanks. Do you know where McGinty lives?"

"No, sorry. But you could ask Maeve. She'll know."

"OK, thanks very much, Adam. We'll let you get back to your computer now. Here's my card if you think of anything else useful," Maguire said, handing him the item.

"Thanks. I hope you catch whoever did this. Conor was a good mate. I'll miss him," Wallace said, trying to hide the tears that were starting to well up in his eyes.

Chapter Fifteen

"Come in, Martin. Sit ye down and tell me where we are with the Nevin murders today," Superintendent O'Connell said, gesturing to the comfy leather chair positioned at the far side of his desk.

O'Shea outlined where they were at with the various strands of the investigation, while Derry O'Connell listened intently, looking ever more unhappy with the detective inspector's report.

"It doesn't look like you've made much progress. That's not good. There are a lot of eyes on us just now. We need to make a good impression."

"Yes, I realize that, sir. But it's only been a few days, and the whole thing is very peculiar. It's going to take a fair bit of digging to unearth the truth here, but we are getting somewhere," O'Shea said rather defensively.

"I'm not sure I agree. There needs to be some very obvious success with this soon, or we're all in the soup. I can't afford to have this drag on. And before you ask, no, I can't get any more resources without handing the whole thing over to another team, and neither of us want that."

"No, of course not, sir."

"Do you think it would help if I sat in on some of your briefings? Lend a bit of gravitas to the occasion, as it were."

O'Shea was taken aback. "Well, of course you're very welcome to attend at any time, sir, obviously, and we would welcome your input, but I don't think you have to. I'll be keeping you well up to date with any developments."

"Did you ever think of joining the diplomatic corps?" O'Connell asked, smiling a wry smile.

"Will there be anything else, sir? I'm keen to get on and follow a new lead that came in last night."

"Off you go then. But remember what I said. Results, Martin, results – and soon!"

* * *

O'Shea wanted to see Dermot Boggan as soon as he could. The man apparently had a motive to harm Pat Nevin, and as his property more or less adjoined the Nevins' farm, he could easily have made off on foot after doing the deed – although, in fairness, it looked as if their killer had actually gone in completely the other direction. But that may have been a deliberate subterfuge.

He took the N59 travelling north-west out of Westport, then turned off at Creggaunnahorna and on through Coolbarreen, which brought him into Mucklagh. He found the narrow road that ran behind the Nevins' farm and drove along until he came across a gate that opened onto a single track with grass and weeds growing up the centre of it. He edged his car in gingerly and drove slowly up the potholed drive that finally opened out into a farmyard covered in small, loose stones. O'Shea stopped the car and spent a few minutes taking in the scene.

The house that stood at one side of the yard was plastered in dull grey cement. It was two stories high, with a pitched slate roof, but some of the slates were missing, exposing the blackened and wet rafters beneath. The wooden windows had flaking paint, and the front door looked to be falling off its hinges with the drab dark-green paint missing around the door lock and handle.

At the other side of the yard, facing the house, stood a corrugated iron barn, open at the front, and O'Shea could see various items of farm machinery that appeared to be rusting quietly away inside. The entire premises had an air of neglect and decay about it.

He got out of the car and went to the front door of the house, rapping three times on the wood, hoping that it wouldn't give way under the pressure. A dog barked within.

After a few minutes, the door was opened, scraping itself back on the concrete stoop. A black-and-white sheepdog greeted O'Shea before a very bedraggled man he presumed was Dermot Boggan appeared in the opening. The man was unshaven and dressed in a collarless shirt, tucked into a pair of greasy grey suit trousers. His shock of red hair was askew, and O'Shea could see that a trip to the dentist was long overdue.

"Are you Dermot Boggan?" O'Shea asked, holding up his warrant card.

"Who the fuck are you?"

"Detective Inspector Martin O'Shea. I need to ask you a few questions. May I come in please?"

"No, you can't. Ask your questions, and be gone with you," Boggan replied gruffly.

"Very well. Can you tell me about your relationship with Pat Nevin?" O'Shea asked, nodding in the direction of the Nevins' farm.

"That blaggard! You know he's stolen my land. It's him you should be questioning, but I suppose you can't now, can you?" Boggan said with a wide toothless grin.

"I'm not here about land ownership, Mr Boggan. Where were you on Monday night, early Tuesday morning?"

"I was in Castlebar at a nightclub getting frisky with a 20-year-old blonde of course. Where do you think I bloody well was?"

"I need you to tell me honestly, Mr Boggan, otherwise I'll have to take you to the Garda station," O'Shea said, not relishing the thought of sharing his car with the man, who smelled a bit ripe.

"For fuck's sake! I was here of course. Where else would I be?"

"Can anyone verify that?"

"Hm. You can ask the dog if you like, but his English isn't the best."

O'Shea's patience was wearing thin. He turned away from the man for a minute to compose himself then turned back to Boggan.

"Look, mate, I'm investigating a double murder, and you just happen to have motive and opportunity from what I can see. So if I were you, I'd cut the wisecracks and just answer my questions honestly. Otherwise, I'll have you arrested on suspicion of murder, and you'll be taken away."

Boggan stopped smirking and stood back from the entrance. "You'd better come in."

O'Shea followed the man inside, down along the hall into the kitchen at the back of the house. The range was going, and the room, although neglected like the rest of the property, was warm.

"Tea?" Boggan asked.

"No, thank you," O'Shea replied as Boggan cleared a space on the table and gestured for the detective to take a seat.

Boggan equipped himself with a mug of strong tea from the brown earthenware teapot that was simmering on the corner of the range and sat opposite O'Shea. "I'm sorry about earlier. You caught me on a bad day."

"OK. So tell me again: what were your dealings with Pat Nevin?"

"There's a field out across the lane from this place that Nevin claims is his. But my father bought it from his father back in the 1980s when the Nevins hit hard times. He gave him a fair price for it, and Nevin was glad to do the deal. It saved him from going bust. But as soon as things improved, Nevin denied the transaction."

"Was there no paperwork exchanged or anything?"

"No, there wasn't. Old man Nevin didn't want all and sundry to know his business, so they just shook hands on it and that was that," Boggan said.

"And what's so important about that particular plot of land?"

"It's the only bit of this holding that has road frontage. I have 45 hectares here, but it's all landlocked. I have a right of way to get in and out through the land you came across when you drove in here, but the fields on either side of the driveway aren't mine. As you can see, I'm not doing too well just now, but if I had that field that Nevin stole, I could get planning permission and sell it for building.

That would see me right. I could get this place sorted out and have a bit over."

"Did you discuss this with Nevin?"

"Sure, of course I did. Every chance I got. But he just kept saying that it was obviously part of their property, and I didn't know what I was talking about. But I'll tell you this: my father was an honest man. He never did anyone out of anything his whole life long, and he swore to me on his death bed that the field was ours, bought and paid for."

"Did you ever threaten Pat Nevin or his family, Mr Boggan?"

"Call me Dermot, Inspector. No one calls me Mr Boggan. And yes, I did. But just words mind, nothing more. Sticks and stones, etc."

"So just to be clear: the night that the Nevins were killed, you were here on your own, probably asleep. You didn't go out at all, and you didn't see or hear anything out of the ordinary. Is that right?"

"It is. Just as you say, and I'll swear to God that's the truth. Have you no idea who killed them, Inspector?"

"We're following a number of enquiries, but we haven't arrested anyone yet."

"It's a scary thing, you know. Us poor farmers stuck out here in the country with no one to look out for us. If there's a madman on the loose killing folk, I could be next."

"I shouldn't worry, Dermot. This looks to us to have been a very targeted affair. I'm sure you're quite safe."

Chapter Sixteen

O'Shea left Boggan's farm and drove back towards Westport. This time, he took the route that led him close to the rugby club, before turning east again onto Golf Course Road. He turned in between the stout stone pillars at the entrance to the golf course and rattled across the cattle grid, driving up through the manicured tree-lined avenue towards the impressive modern clubhouse.

There were just a handful of cars parked in front of the building, and looking around, O'Shea could see very few players out on the course itself. The yellow flags marking the pins on the holes nearest to where he was parked fluttered gently in the breeze.

O'Shea entered a very high and spacious atrium where a sort of reception desk was fixed into one of the side walls. Behind the counter that it supported, an array of trophies was housed in glass-fronted cabinets, and a display board giving the names of the various captains of the club in gold lettering was positioned off to one side. A young woman was seated behind the desk and greeted him as he approached.

"Good morning," she said, smiling. "How may I help you?"

O'Shea held out his warrant card for her to examine. "Hello. My name is DI Martin O'Shea from Westport Gardaí. I got a message that the secretary was looking to speak to me."

The girl said nothing, but lifted the receiver on her telephone and made a call. A moment later, she looked up, smiling again. "Mr Webster will be with you in a minute. Would you like to wait in the lounge? You can get a tea or a coffee in there."

"Thanks," O'Shea said and strolled into the lounge, where a young man was busy restocking the bar.

O'Shea walked over to the huge windows that gave a superb view of much of the golf course and took a seat on a grey tweed-covered sofa facing outwards. He didn't have long to wait.

Webster was dressed in a smart navy suit with a pale yellow shirt and a club tie. He had highly polished black leather shoes and an erect posture. He walked purposefully over to where his guest was seated, extending his hand as he approached.

O'Shea got up and shook hands with the man. "Mr Webster. Nice to meet you. You were looking for me earlier. I was out this way, so I thought it would be just as handy to call in. It's a lovely facility you have here."

"Thank you. We do our best. Please be seated. May I offer you a tea or a coffee?"

"No, thanks. I can't stop. Lots going on."

"Ah, yes. That's why I wanted to have a word. You see, we've had a bit of vandalism here at the club recently. Some exuberant youths on quad bikes have taken to coming in and riding over the greens in the middle of the night. Makes a right mess, I can tell you. So we've been experimenting with some CCTV near the entrance in the hope of catching and identifying the little buggers," Webster said.

"I'm sorry to hear that, Mr Webster. Have you spoken to our uniformed people about it?"

"Oh, yes, but that's not why I wanted to speak to you. The cameras we've installed are quite sophisticated. They have full night vision, and they're motion-sensor activated. And on the night that those poor people were killed out at Mucklagh, we recorded a motorcycle going past the entrance in the wee small hours, heading back towards Westport. I thought it might be of some use to you."

"Yes, indeed it could be. That's very civic minded of you. Do you have a copy of the footage?"

"I have. I transferred it onto this little thumb drive for you," Webster said, offering a tiny black device to O'Shea. "I've had a look, and I can't make out an awful lot, to be honest, but your technical people may be able to enhance it. He had no lights on or anything."

"I'm sure it will be a great help. To be frank, we're not finding this case easy. Anything that can throw some light on the matter could be very useful. Thanks again."

"You're welcome, Inspector. And if I may be so bold, perhaps you could have a word with your uniformed colleagues about the vandalism. You have no idea how costly, not to say inconvenient, it is to have to repair our greens," Webster said.

"Yes, of course. I'll do just that. How often has it happened?"

"Twice in the last six weeks, and of course the quad bikes have no registration plates or anything, so it's impossible to trace who owns them that way."

"Yes, of course. Anyway, I must be getting on. Thanks again for the footage, and I'll have a word for you."

"Excellent. Thanks, Inspector."

The two of them walked in silence to the door where they shook hands again, and then O'Shea was off back to the station.

* * *

Agnes Gallagher had no difficulty finding an address for James McGinty because he was in the Garda PULSE system. He'd been given a caution after he'd got involved in an affray in Sligo with another young man. McGinty had taken exception to some comment made at a house party, and fisticuffs had ensued. But witnesses said that McGinty was the troublemaker, and he'd been carted off to the Garda station and given a severe talking-to and a formal caution.

The address was in Sligo, which Gallagher suspected was the family home. It didn't take her long to source a phone number for the McGinty house, and she made the call. The phone was answered by a female after four rings.

"Yes?" the woman said.

"Good morning. Is that Mrs McGinty?"

"Yes. Who's this please?"

"My name is Detective Garda Agnes Gallagher from Westport. I'm trying to contact James McGinty. Is he there please?"

"Is that James senior or junior?"

"It's the student who's attending ATU in Westport. Is he there please?"

Gallagher knew that he probably wasn't at home, but she didn't want his mother to have too much thinking time before replying.

"No, he's not here. He stays in Westport during the week. He has a room in a house there near the college. What has he done now?" the woman asked, sounding a little exasperated.

"I just need to speak to him regarding an ongoing enquiry. Can you give me his address please?"

"Hold on. I'll go and get it," she said, putting down the telephone receiver.

Gallagher could hear the woman retreating, and in a few moments, she was back.

"Hello. Yes, here it is. He rents a room on St Patrick's Terrace. It's near the college. The couple who live there are empty nesters, and they're glad of the money for the room."

"Do you have a number of the house, Mrs McGinty?"

"Oh, sorry, yes, it's number 22."

"And do you know the name of the owners of the house?"

"Eh, wait now, yes, I think they are Mr and Mrs Byrne. Yes, that's right, I remember now."

"Right. Thanks, Mrs McGinty."

Gallagher knew the location that Mrs McGinty had given her. It was a good fifteen minutes' walk, so she decided to take a marked squad car, which, she felt, would look more official in any case.

She arrived at St Patrick's Terrace after the short drive. The street was one way and entered off Quay Road. The houses were in long terraces on both sides, and although they looked as if they may at one time have been local-authority properties, they were now quite obviously privately owned. Some of the residents had sacrificed the small front gardens to provide off-street parking for one car in front of their house, which wasn't a bad idea, as the street was quite narrow.

Number 22 was one such property, and a nearly new Toyota Yaris in gleaming bright red was availing of the facility.

At least it looks as if someone is at home, Gallagher thought as she parked half up on the footpath so as not to obstruct through traffic.

When she rang the doorbell, a small, elderly woman answered the door. She was a little bit stooped but otherwise seemed to be in reasonable condition. Gallagher judged her to be in her late seventies or maybe even her eighties.

"Good morning, ma'am. I'm Detective Garda Gallagher, and I'm looking to speak to James McGinty. He does live here, doesn't he?"

"Some of the time, yes. But he's not here at the minute. Is he in trouble?" the woman asked, as if she was expecting that to be the case.

"No, not at all. I just need to ask him a few questions about an ongoing investigation. What time will he be back at?"

The woman rolled her eyes to heaven. "God knows. He comes and goes as he pleases. More of a nuisance than anything else, he is. He wakes us up most nights. I wish he was gone out of here."

"I see. I'm sorry to hear that. Do you think he might be in college?"

"I don't know, Guard, and to be honest with you, I

don't much care. He might be, I suppose. Why don't you go across and ask them?"

Gallagher thought for a moment. She wasn't sure if she left her details that McGinty would contact her, and if he had been involved with the crime out at the Nevins' farm, it might spook him to the point where he took off.

"Yes, maybe I'll do that. If you see him before I do, don't mention I was looking for him, will you?"

"Fair enough."

"Thanks. Sorry, I didn't catch your name," Gallagher said.

"Byrne. Mrs Byrne."

"Great, well thanks, Mrs Byrne. I'll leave you in peace now."

Chapter Seventeen

Gallagher didn't relish the thought of searching all over the ATU campus for James McGinty, but she felt she had to follow it up, especially as some of the neighbours might have seen the Garda car at number 22 and inform McGinty.

She drove back to the college campus and went inside, where she met the grey man she'd heard about from the others detectives and asked for James McGinty.

"Not here. Haven't seen him for a few days," the man said.

Gallagher was impressed with the man's knowledge of individual students, considering there were so many of them attending the college, so she decided to press him a little further. "Can you recall exactly when you did see him last?"

The man gave Gallagher a rather withering look and consulted a large hardback notebook he had open on his desk. "Last week. Friday."

"Do you mind me asking how you know that level of detail? After all, as I understand it, there are several hundred students here."

"His tutor asked me to keep an eye out for him. His attendance has been very patchy, and it goes towards his final grades. Anyway, he's easy to spot with that shock of red hair."

"Ah, OK, thanks."

This time, Gallagher decided to leave her details. "If he does turn up, don't say anything to him, but I'd be obliged if you'd give me a call." She handed him a business card.

"Right, so."

Gallagher left and returned to the Garda station.

* * *

Back in the station, O'Shea asked the troops to gather around. There was some new information he was anxious to share.

"Right, everyone, listen up. Liam had a call from Kevin Walsh in forensics. They thought they'd finished with Nevin's jeep, but just as they were putting it back in the yard, one of the officers found something in the back. It was tucked into the pouch behind the passenger's seat. Apparently, the receptacle is a very tight fit, and they didn't think there was anything in it till this fella spotted it."

"What is it, boss?" Maguire asked.

"That's the thing. It's a hard drive."

"Wow! Have we got it here?"

"No, not yet. They're processing it now. You know, fingerprints and so on. Kevin's going to drop it over later on. Agnes, when it gets here, can you get busy with it? It could be very relevant, given that Conor was so precious about all that data he was allegedly working on."

"Yes, sure, boss. I'll use the stand-alone PC in case there's malware or viruses on the drive."

Then Gallagher remembered the news she had to impart to the team. "Oh, I nearly forgot. James McGinty seems to have gone walkabout. He's not in his digs, or at home, and he hasn't been in college for a few days either."

"I see," O'Shea said. "Can someone call Maeve Kilcoyne and see if she's heard from him? If not, we'd better circulate his photograph and ask the force to be on the lookout for him. Just as a person of interest. We don't need to arrest him or anything."

"I'll look after that, boss," Maguire said.

"Thanks, Deirdre. Now, in other news, I paid a visit to Nevin's neighbour, Dermot Boggan, earlier. Not much there. I don't think he's a double murderer. But on the way back, I called at the golf club, and the secretary gave me a thumb drive with some footage from the night of the killings." O'Shea held the drive up. "This contains a clip of a motorcycle speeding past the golf club entrance in the early hours. Agnes, while you're waiting for the hard drive, can you have a look and see if there's anything useful on it?"

"Of course. Give it here," Gallagher said.

She took the tiny device and turned it over in the palm of her hand.

"Right. Let's get busy. I'm going upstairs to give O'Connell the news that we're moving forward to keep him off our backs," O'Shea said.

The little group dispersed to go about their assigned tasks.

Gallagher took the thumb drive across to the PC that wasn't connected to the network, booted it up and inserted the device into one of the free USB slots. At once, an icon for the new device appeared on the screen.

Gallagher double-clicked on it, and it opened to reveal several video files. She powered up the VLC program and opened the first file. The image was a bit fuzzy, but after a few seconds, she saw what O'Shea had reported. A motorbike went past the golf-club gates from left to right. It had no lights on, but the lights from the club entrance were reflected by the number plate, which looked to be pale yellow.

Gallagher called Deirdre Maguire over. "Look at this, Sarge. It's definitely doing some speed, and the timestamp says 3:55 a.m. That ties in with the approximate time of the killings as far as we know."

"Back it up and run it through again very slowly, Agnes. Stop it when we have the best view of the back of the bike."

Gallagher clicked the arrow keys on the keyboard, and the video clip rewound. The motorbike appeared to be travelling backwards till it was out of the frame, and then, as Gallagher pressed another key, the bike reappeared.

"Stop it there," Maguire said. "Can you see the number plate?"

Gallagher tapped a few more keys, and the image magnified. They could see that the number plate was yellow, but it was impossible to read any of the digits.

"Does that look like a UK plate to you, Agnes?"

"Could be, Sarge. But we're never going to get any detail from this. Maybe if I email it to the Technical Bureau up in Dublin, they may be able to get something off it. What do you think?" Gallagher asked.

"Good idea. But be sure to keep the original here. You might be able to do something yourself with it."

"Yes, of course."

Chapter Eighteen

A short while later, the desk sergeant rang Maguire to say there was a package for her. She retrieved the padded envelope from the front desk and came back upstairs. Agnes Gallagher was still at her desk, rolling the video clip from the golf club back and forth without any apparent success.

"Hi, Agnes. This is the hard drive that was found in the Nevins' car. Can you take charge of it for me? I suggest the first thing you do is clone it and put the original into the evidence room," Maguire said.

"OK, Sarge. Did they get any prints off it?"

"Yes, but just Conor's. Nothing else."

"I'll have to go out and buy another disk to copy this one onto. I have the software, but I don't have a disk of that capacity. They'll probably have one in that Chinese phone shop on James Street. If not, I'll have to run into Castlebar. Do you want to hang on to it till I get back?"

"Yes, OK. I'll give it to DI O'Shea for safekeeping."

Gallagher put on her coat and set off on her mission, while Maguire took the original into O'Shea's office.

"Hi. How's it going?" she asked her boss.

"Hi, Deirdre. Not much further on, I'm afraid. I've been doing a bit of digging into the Nevins' finances.

I got on to the bank. Strictly speaking, I should have a warrant, but I know the manager, so he gave me the edited highlights on the quiet."

"Nice. Anything useful?"

"Well, they weren't very flush. In fact, they were quite a bit overdrawn, but Matt said that's not unusual for beef farmers at this time of year. Once the cattle are sold off, it usually clears down the debt and leaves a good bit over to tide them through the winter. But he said Nevin would need to do very well at the market to clear all that he owed, and head office were getting a bit uneasy about it."

"I see. So if Pat Nevin and his son could come up with some caper that would earn them a nice little stash, that would have been very handy," Maguire said.

"Yes, it would. Very handy indeed."

"That could explain the clandestine nature of their nocturnal activities. But I wonder what was in that damn bag that was so important. It wasn't drugs by all accounts. Oh, this is the disk forensics found in Nevin's jeep. Can you mind it till Agnes gets back? She's gone to find a blank one to copy it on to."

"Good idea. Hopefully it'll reveal something of interest, but yes, I'll lock it in my desk drawer in the meantime."

* * *

Agnes Gallagher was fortunate. The Chinese phone shop did indeed have a USB drive of similar capacity to the one they'd found and was delighted to sell it to her for what seemed like quite a modest sum. She was back in the station 20 minutes later and asked Maguire for the one they hoped might unlock the key to their mystery.

Armed with both disks, plugged into separate USB ports on the standalone PC, Gallagher fired up the cloning software and set about making an exact replica of the original disk. The process took nearly half an hour, and Gallagher stood over it, watching as it progressed, in case it stopped working for any reason. When the dialogue on the screen finally announced that it had completed, she carefully dismounted the two disk drives and stuck a label on the new disk, identifying it as a copy of the original retrieved from the crime scene vehicle. She then placed the original into an evidence bag and labelled it as well.

Gallagher then opened the cloned disk and started to explore. There were several folders, all clearly labelled with titles such as "sample 1", "sample 2" and so on, and several others labelled with odd names that Gallagher didn't understand but which clearly meant something to Conor Nevin. The folders contained a mixture of Excel spreadsheets, Word documents and JPEG files. Some of the spreadsheets were very large – so much so that the PC she was working on couldn't open them. But others were more manageable, and she was able to view all the Word documents without issue.

Gallagher had been studying the contents of the disk for over an hour when Maguire approached.

"Anything interesting, Agnes?"

"Loads. There's masses of data that seems to be connected to bacteria counts in milk samples and cheese. I don't really understand it, but I've found a few documents that set out a summary of the analysis. There's a good bit of talk about a substance called inulin, and there's a reference to a local cheese maker here in town – Westport Way Cheese."

"Cripes! You're making me hungry. Are you OK to keep going with this and see if you can get to some kind of conclusion?" Maguire asked.

"Yes, but I might need to call for some help. I'm no scientist."

"That's fine. Maybe someone from forensics can give you a hand, or if you get really stuck, there's always the college?"

"Yes, OK. I'll just grab a quick sandwich and keep going then."

* * *

After Gallagher left, Maguire's mobile rang. She looked at the screen and saw it was a landline number she didn't recognize. She took the call.

"Miss Maguire, this is the administrator at ATU where Conor Nevin was in attendance. We spoke yesterday. I've come across something that may be of interest, but I'd rather not discuss it on the telephone. Would you happen to be passing this way today at all?"

"Oh, hello. Yes, I could do, but can you give me an idea of what you've found?" Maguire asked.

"It would be best if we wait until you're here. It's not easy to explain."

"OK, I'll pop out shortly then. Will you be there all afternoon?"

"I'm going to take my lunch break now, but I'll be back at my desk in half an hour."

"Right. I'll see you shortly then."

Maguire finished the call then held the phone away from her face and frowned at it. "How odd," she said to nobody and put the phone back in her jacket pocket.

Chapter Nineteen

Maguire had brought Liam Staunton with her for the drive around to the ATU campus. She wasn't sure what she was about to encounter, and she figured that another pair of eyes and ears would be helpful.

It was starting to rain as they made their way towards the college, and Maguire hoped she'd be able to park near the entrance. She had no waterproof clothing with her.

Luckily, she found just such a spot when they arrived. "Ready to make a run for it?" Maguire asked Staunton.

The rain had become considerably heavier, and it was now chucking it down.

Once inside, the detectives shook as much rainwater from their clothes as they could and approached the man at the desk.

"Hello, Sergeant. I'll be with you in a minute," he said.

Maguire and Staunton stood patiently observing the throng of students passing by on their way to various lectures.

Eventually, the man looked up from what he was doing.

"Now. One of my jobs here is to manage the printing and photocopying at the college. Each student has a card, and when they need to print something or make copies, they insert the card into a slot on the machine they're using. The card records the number of pages printed or copied, along with some other details, and we charge the students at the end of the month for their usage. They have a basic allowance of 100 pages, but after that, they pay three cents per page."

Maguire looked at the man, somewhat puzzled.

"What may be of interest is that Conor Nevin printed some 800 pages off during the night recently, and I think it may have been the night that he was killed."

"Wow! Does the system record what was printed – apart from the number of pages, that is?" Staunton asked.

"Not exactly. It tells us which server the material was stored on but not any details of the substance of the files. But what's even more peculiar is that all the stuff that was printed has now been deleted. I spoke to our network operator, and she confirmed that it's gone. Not a trace."

"Could we speak to this person?" Maguire asked.

"Yes, of course. But as I told you, whatever Conor had on the server has now disappeared. Hold on – I'll ask her to come down."

The man dialled a number and spoke briefly into the phone.

"What's this woman's name, sir?" Staunton asked.

"Mary Claffey. She's actually a student here too, but she gets paid to mind the IT stuff as well."

A few minutes later, a young woman dressed in the universal student attire of blue jeans and a dark sweater approached. She had dark shoulder-length hair and a cheerful, round face.

"Hi. I'm Mary. You wanted to speak to me?"

"Hello, Mary," Maguire said and introduced her colleague. "We wanted to ask you about Conor Nevin's research material that he had on your servers here at the college."

"Oh, yes, poor Conor. That was dreadful what happened to him. What do you want to know?"

"We've been told that Conor printed off a whole lot of material here during the night and then deleted it off your servers. Is that correct?"

"Yes, well nearly. He did print masses of information all right, but he didn't delete it. Someone else did."

Maguire looked at Staunton.

"I see. Do you know who that was and when it was deleted?" Staunton asked.

"Yes. It was Adam Wallace, and it was done the morning after Conor was killed."

"But how can that happen? Surely each student's stuff is protected from the other students?" Maguire said.

"Yes, it is normally. Conor must have given Adam his password or something. It's very odd."

"What about a backup copy? I presume you back up all the students' work every day?" Staunton asked.

Mary's face reddened. "I know we should. But we're pretty strapped for cash in the IT department, and we haven't enough storage to keep the backups, so they're overwritten every two nights. Conor's files will be gone by now."

"Terrific!" Staunton said.

"I'm sorry. It's not my fault. I do my best," Mary said, tearing up a little.

"It's OK, Mary. I know it's not your fault. Don't worry. Is Adam here today?" Maguire asked.

"Yes. He's in the computer lab. Do you want to talk to him?"

"Yes, please. Could you ask him to come down for a minute?"

Adam presented himself as requested a few minutes later.

"Adam, Mary tells us that you deleted all Conor's files from the server the morning after he was found. Is that right?"

"Yes, but I didn't know he'd been killed at that time, did I?" he said, obviously a little flustered by the question.

"Why did you delete the files?" Staunton asked.

"Conor left me a note asking me to do it. He said it was really important and to do it as soon as I got in. He said to make sure all his files were off the server. So I did it. It was a strange request, but we were good mates, so I just did as he asked. Did I do something wrong?"

Maguire paused for a moment before responding. "No, you didn't. It's a pity, but it's not your fault. I presume you had Conor's password then?"

Adam looked around a little sheepishly. "Yes. And he had mine too. I know it's not strictly within the rules, but as I said, we were good mates."

Maguire let Adam go back to his work, then they thanked the administrator for his help and left the college.

On the way back to the car, Staunton said, "God give me strength! What a fiasco. Good job we have the disk from the car. But why didn't Conor delete his own stuff? This thing is wrecking my head!"

"Isn't it just, Liam? Let's get back and see what Agnes has made of it all."

Chapter Twenty

Martin O'Shea brought the entire team together late in the afternoon for a meeting.

"Well, everyone, what have we discovered today?"

Maguire recounted the visit they'd made to the college campus and what they'd learned.

"That's interesting. So it looks as if Conor Nevin may have discovered something in his research that could just possibly be what got him killed. Anyone any ideas?"

Agnes Gallagher spoke up. "I've spent most of the day going through the mountain of data that was on the disk we found in the car. I'm not finished yet, and I need to get a microbiologist to confirm what I think I've found, but it appears that Conor discovered that there's something wrong with a substance called inulin. It's used as a bulking agent in the manufacture of some cheeses. According to one of the papers I read, Conor discovered that the inulin, which comes from the Far East, could be contaminated with some pretty nasty stuff. He'd prepared a paper on it that he was going to have published. There are a number of drafts on the disk."

"I see," O'Shea said. "Do we think that could have been enough to have him silenced?"

"Possibly," Maguire said, "and all this business about

printing it off in the middle of the night looks as if he was scared of something. He wasn't wrong, was he?"

"OK, let's talk scenarios. Conor Nevin discovers that there's a problem with this inulin stuff. Somehow, the word gets out that he's about to go public with it, and either the supplier of the product, or someone who's using it in their cheese can't afford for that to happen," O'Shea said.

"But would that be enough to get him killed, boss? Surely not."

"You just never know with these things. We need more information. Agnes, are you OK to stay on this? Find out as much as you can about this inulin. Who supplies it. Who uses it. How much of it is imported into Ireland and anything else you can. OK?"

"Yes, sir. I may have to ask for help though," Gallagher said.

"OK, but try to keep it tight until we run out of road. If there is something in this theory, heaven knows who may be involved."

"There is one avenue we could explore, sir," Gallagher said.

"Oh. What's that?"

"There's a local cheese-making outfit that was mentioned in a couple of the papers Conor wrote. It's Westport Way Cheese. I've never heard of them, but it looks like they're here in town – or nearby."

"Right. Deirdre, can you follow up with that? Go and see them. Find out if they're actually using inulin currently, and if so, where they get it," O'Shea said.

"Right, boss. I'll get to it tomorrow first thing."

"Anything more on the video we got from the golf

club?" O'Shea asked.

"No, nothing, sir. I sent it up to the Technical Bureau to see if they could enhance it. I'll follow it up tomorrow too."

"Great, thanks. OK, let's call it quits for the day. There's lots to do tomorrow. Deirdre, could you hold on for a few minutes?"

"Yes, of course, boss."

Maguire wondered what was coming at her. She had a good relationship with O'Shea, but he was her boss after all.

When the others had dispersed, he beckoned her into his office. She couldn't stand the suspense any longer, so she asked, "What's up boss?"

"Oh, nothing, really. I just wanted to find out how you're getting on. Tell you what – why don't we go for a drink?"

"Yes, OK. Give me a minute to freshen up. I'll see you downstairs."

"Yes, fine."

Maguire went to the ladies and combed her hair and checked her make-up. Her curiosity had been piqued. What did O'Shea want from her?

The two of them went to Joyce's pub. O'Shea went to the bar and ordered a pint of Guinness for himself and a vodka and tonic for Maguire. He was back at their table a few minutes later.

"*Sláinte*!" he said, clinking glasses with Maguire, who was growing more curious by the minute.

"So what's on your mind, boss?" she asked a little tentatively.

"Ah, nothing much, Deirdre, and call me Martin

when we're not working. I just wanted to see how you're settling in to the new arrangements. How you're getting on with the team, that sort of thing."

"To be honest, I haven't really had time to think too much about everything what with this case. But things are going OK. Agnes and Liam seem keen enough, if a little inexperienced. But they'll get there in time. What do you think of them?"

"Which one would you rather have beside you if you were in a tight spot?" he responded, dodging the question.

"Agnes, for sure. She's very quick-witted, and I'd say she could be a tough cookie too."

"Yes, I agree. She has a bit of a track record in that regard. She overpowered a nasty piece of work last year when she was out on patrol. Some dope was using his girlfriend as a punchbag outside a pub in Castlebar, and Agnes put him on the ground and handcuffed him. But in the end, the woman wouldn't press charges, so he had to be let go."

"Wow! Remind me not to fall out with her then," Maguire said, smiling and taking a sip of her drink.

"What about you, Martin? How are you finding things here?"

"It's all a bit new just yet. And the super is expecting miracles. He wants to use this posting to climb up the greasy pole, so he's relying on us to get results. But there's nothing new about that scenario. The missus is enjoying being back here though, and you know what they say – 'happy wife, happy life'. On the subject of which, is there anyone special in your orbit right now?"

Maguire wasn't entirely comfortable with the question, but she replied all the same. "I am seeing someone. It's not very serious, but we get along OK," she said.

"Is it going anywhere?" O'Shea asked.

"We'll see."

"Playing it close to your chest, then,"

"It's not that, boss. It's just I'm not sure exactly what either of us want from the relationship just yet. But he's a nice fella. I'll give it a bit more time, and see how it goes."

"Fair enough. You don't want to rush into these things and then regret it later. I'm sure you'll figure it out in any case," O'Shea said.

They chatted for a few more minutes before Maguire felt she could politely say, "I'd better be getting off now. I've a pile of housework waiting for me."

She knocked back the remainder of her drink, gathered up her handbag and coat, and said goodbye to her boss.

Chapter Twenty-One

The team had been allocated their tasks the previous evening at the station, so the following morning, they were all busy. Agnes Gallagher was continuing the work she'd started on the information from the USB hard drive found in the Nevins' car while she waited for the Technical Bureau to get back to her with any further information they could extract from the golf-club's video clip.

Meanwhile, Deirdre Maguire went to visit Westport Way Cheese. The cheese-making facility was housed in a large green metal construction beside a tidy-looking dairy farmhouse on the east side of Westport near Dooncastle just off the R309. The driveway up to the house, and its associated outbuildings, was bordered by wooden stud fencing and had been rendered in fresh tarmacadam with concrete edging. It gave the appearance of being well tended and prosperous. Maguire pulled her car up in front of the house and got out. It was a bright day, with just a few fluffy clouds high in the sky, although it was cool at just ten degrees centigrade.

She walked towards the large shed and was met by a woman coming out carrying a large blue plastic tray, dressed in a long white coat and blue hairnet, and wearing blue vinyl gloves.

"Can I help you?" the woman called as Maguire approached.

"Hello. My name is Detective Sergeant Maguire from Westport Gardaí," she said, holding up her warrant card. "I wonder if I could speak to the manager please?"

"There's no managers here, Guard. I'm the owner, Mrs Blenerhassett. Will I do?"

"Oh, right. Would you have a few minutes, Mrs Blenerhassett? I need to ask you some questions."

"If we can walk and talk. I have to get this order out before half past ten."

"Sure." Maguire fell in step with the woman, who carried the tray of cheeses to a waiting small white van with a refrigeration unit on the roof and Westport Way Cheese painted on its side in green script.

"So how can I help you?" the woman asked when she'd deposited the tray alongside several others in the back of the van and closed the door.

"I'm interested in the process by which you make the cheese. Can I ask what exactly goes into it?"

Mrs Blenerhassett looked askance at Maguire. "That's a funny question. Milk of course. That's it."

"Are there're no additives, like colouring or anything?"

"No, of course not, unless you count salt."

"Do you ever use a bulking agent in the cheese?" Maguire pressed on.

Blenerhassett said nothing and continued to organize the cargo in the back of the van, so Maguire said, "Well, Mrs Blenerhassett?"

"We use a small amount of inulin in one or two of the varieties. It helps to bind the cheese and makes it go a bit further, but it's only used in very small quantities."

Blenerhassett closed the van door and started off walking back to the shed.

"I wonder if I could have a small sample of it?"

The woman stopped and turned to face Maguire. "Look, what's all this about?"

"I'd just like to take away a sample of the inulin, if that's all right. I don't need much. Where does it come from?"

"We get it from the Netherlands, but it's made in the Far East. It's all natural ingredients from plants. There's nothing wrong with it. We could use another synthetic product that would be much cheaper, but I don't like the idea. I want to keep our product pure."

"I understand," Maguire said. They were back inside the cheese-making plant now, and Maguire was impressed by the cleanliness of the place, and the seemingly acres of gleaming stainless steel, including two huge silos with blue pipes connected to them near the base.

"This is quite an undertaking. I'm impressed," Maguire said.

"You should have seen how we started out. Just a few old saucepans in the kitchen and milk absolutely everywhere. That was six years ago. We've come a long way."

"So if I could just have a small tub of the inulin, then I'll leave you in peace."

Mrs Blenerhassett went to the corner of the area where three white bags were stacked on top of each other. The bags had blue writing on them with a company name and "inulin" in large letters. Beneath the word inulin was "approved for food use" and some sort of circular stamp that might have come from a regulatory authority.

Blenerhassett opened the top bag and took a scoop of the creamy-coloured powder. She put the lid on the small tub she'd filled and handed it to Maguire.

"Thanks. That's all I need for now. If there's anything else, we will be in touch."

"May I give you a sample of our cheese?" Blenerhassett asked.

"Better not, thanks. It could be misinterpreted."

"Oh, right, sorry."

Maguire walked back out to her car and placed the tub of powder on the passenger's seat. She drove back briskly to the Garda station. She didn't really like cheese in any case.

Chapter Twenty-Two

His phone vibrated in his pocket. He took it out and looked at the screen, but there was no indication of who was on the other end of the call.

"Yes," he said.

"We got the bag, but it's only paperwork. We need the electronic copies too."

"You mean you didn't check?"

"No. I just wanted to get out of there and get it back to you as quickly as possible."

"We need the rest. I'm not paying you a red cent till we have the originals on disk. And you'd better make sure there are no copies either."

"I can't do that. God knows where they are by now. The cops could even have them."

"Not my problem. Just do it." The phone went dead.

He tried to call the number back, but it had been disconnected already. These people didn't mess around.

Chapter Twenty-Three

When Maguire got back to the Garda station, she carried her precious tub of inulin carefully to her desk. Then she called Agnes Gallagher over.

"I got the inulin, and I need you to get it away to a laboratory somewhere. We need a very full analysis of exactly what it contains, and I want it done quietly. Can you handle that?"

"I guess so. I have a friend that works at that big pharma company over in Sligo. I could give her a call and see if she can get it organized. She's always prattling on about how clever their scientists are and what amazing facilities they have."

"Great. See if you can sort it then. By the way, is there any news on James McGinty?"

"Gosh, no, sorry, boss. He slipped my mind, I'm afraid, with everything else that's going on."

"OK. Well, get Liam to do a check around to see if anyone has seen him anywhere, and then give the place he's staying a call and see if he's turned up there. Is the DI in?"

"Yes, he's just popped upstairs for a few minutes. He shouldn't be long. Hang on – talk of the devil!" Gallagher said.

O'Shea came in and went to his office with Maguire following close behind.

"Morning, boss. Any developments?" Maguire asked.

"Hi, Deirdre. Yes, there are. Agnes got word back from the Technical Bureau about the golf-course CCTV. They've managed to unscramble the number plate on the motorbike. It's a UK number, but they only have a partial. Apparently, the tax disc was arranged to obscure some of the digits. But there might be enough. They also confirmed the make of the bike. It's a Honda Pan European. Agnes is going to call the DVLA and see if they can help to identify the registered owner."

"Bit of a long shot, isn't it, boss?"

"Maybe. But we can but try. What about you – any joy at the cheese place?"

"Yes, I got a sample of the inulin. Agnes is going to get it sent off to the lab."

"Good! Listen, I think we need to go back out to the Nevins' place. I want to ask the wife a few more questions about what the men were doing out at that hour of the night. And while I'm doing that, can you take the FLO outside and grill her? See if she's picked up anything useful."

"Yes, OK. Do you want to go now?"

"No time like the present."

* * *

On the short journey from Westport Garda station to Mucklagh, Maguire phoned back to her team while O'Shea was driving.

"Hi, Agnes. Any luck with your friend in the pharma company?"

"Yes, I've spoken to her, and I'm going to get the inulin driven over to her later. She says she can have it analysed for us. She's dating one of the chemists out there, so it's not a problem."

"Great. Well done. Thanks. See you later."

"Yeah, see ya."

By the time she'd finished the call, they were driving up the narrow track towards the Nevins' farmhouse. They got out and went to the door, which was answered by Mrs Nevin's sister, Bridget Mulligan.

"Hello, Inspector," she said. "Won't you come in?"

O'Shea and Maguire followed the woman along the narrow hallway to the kitchen, which was warm and cosy with a welcoming smell of baked cakes.

"I suppose you know Aisling. She's been great. Eileen is very grateful to have her popping in every day."

Aisling Crotty, the family liaison officer who'd been appointed to help the Nevins overcome their tragedy, was a tall, slim blonde in her late twenties. Her shoulder-length hair was arranged in a ponytail, and she was dressed in snug-fitting black trousers and a black top. She stood up from the table when the detectives entered the room.

"Hello, Aisling. We haven't met. I'm DI Martin O'Shea, and this is DS Deirdre Maguire," O'Shea said, shaking the woman's hand.

Bridget Mulligan was quick to offer them refreshments. "Can I get you a cup of tea, Inspector? And we have some fresh scones just coming out of the oven."

"No, thanks, Mrs Mulligan. I was hoping to have a quick word with Mrs Nevin," O'Shea said, and when Bridget turned away, he nodded to Maguire.

"Aisling, why don't we go outside for a few minutes? Give the inspector some room to talk to the ladies."

"Yes, of course," Aisling said and headed for the door, followed by Maguire.

Bridget Mulligan opened the oven and withdrew a tray of delicious-looking scones, and placed them on the worktop.

"Eileen's just having a rest at the minute, Inspector, but I can get her up if you like?"

"No, no, it's fine, thanks. How has she been?"

"As you'd expect. She's devastated. And it doesn't help that that Boggan man has been calling around pestering her about some land or other he claims to own. He has no consideration, that man."

"Has he called more than once?"

"He has that. But I've sent him packing, and I told him not to come back, or I'd get Shane to see him off."

O'Shea smiled. "Has Mrs Nevin said any more about the night that Pat and Conor were killed?"

"Not really. She did say something one evening that didn't make any sense to me, but she's been very distraught altogether. It's probably not important."

"What was that then?"

"She said she had a bad feeling that Conor was going to get into trouble over something he'd discovered in college. That's all. And maybe she was right."

"I take it she didn't elaborate?"

"No, she didn't, and with the state of her, I didn't want to press it."

"What about yourself, Mrs Mulligan? Will you be staying here much longer?"

"No. I'll have to get back tomorrow. My husband needs me back at home. He's not much of a housekeeper. But I think that girl Aisling will be here a while yet, or so she says. And Shane is very strong. He'll look after his mam."

O'Shea made his excuses and left Bridget Mulligan to her work in the kitchen. Outside, Maguire and Aisling were just finishing their chat too. O'Shea and Maguire bid the family liaison officer goodbye and got back into the car.

"We need to go and see Dermot Boggan again. I'm not having him pestering that poor woman over a bloody patch of land. It's not right."

O'Shea filled Maguire in on the issue of the disputed title to the field at the back of the Nevins' farm as they drove around to Dermot Boggan's place.

"I'm not going to hold back with this fella, Deirdre, so don't get a fright."

"Don't worry, boss. I know what you're like!"

Chapter Twenty-Four

They pulled into the rough yard in front of Dermot Boggan's house. O'Shea hopped out of the car and went to the door, which he struck so hard that Maguire feared it might cave in. O'Shea waited a moment then repeated the assault on the door. Shouting could be heard from within.

"Hold on, hold on. Jesus! Where's the fire?"

Boggan opened the door. His shock of red hair was askew, and he had a couple of days' growth on his face. His clothes were crumpled and dirty, and he looked more like a tramp than a farmer.

"Mr Boggan. You remember me. I'm DI O'Shea, and I've come here to give you a serious warning," O'Shea said with a determined and loud voice. He moved in closer to Boggan so that his face was just inches from the man.

"You stay away from the Nevins. You don't go to their house. You don't go on their land, and you don't communicate with any of them by any means whatsoever. Do I make myself clear?"

"I don't know what you're talking about, Inspector. What have they said?"

"You heard me, Mr Boggan. No contact. No visits. No nothing. If I hear that you've ignored my warning,

I'll have you arrested for harassment. And I can tell you, Dermot Boggan, you wouldn't enjoy the hospitality at Westport nick! Clear?" he shouted in the man's face with such venom that a drop of spittle landed on Boggan's cheek.

Maguire watched on from a few steps away. She couldn't help but be amused at her boss's antics. He was quite impressive when he was riled.

O'Shea stomped off and got back into the car, slamming the door behind him. Maguire slid in the passenger's side, then O'Shea started the engine, revved it loudly and spun the wheels, spraying gravel all over the place as he drove out of the yard.

"You don't think Boggan had anything to do with the killing then?" Maguire asked.

"What do you think? I doubt if he could slice a loaf of bread without cutting himself, never mind clinically see off two healthy specimens like the Nevins. No, he's not our man. But I won't have him intimidating Eileen Nevin in her state. Little shit."

"OK, I get the message, now calm down a bit before you drive us off the road."

O'Shea reduced his speed and sat back in his seat, loosening his iron-like grip on the steering wheel. "Sorry. But he bloody winds me up."

"It's fine – no worries."

* * *

Maguire leaned over Agnes Gallagher's shoulder as the young detective sat at her computer. "Anything new?"

"Yes, Sarge. The DVLA got back to us about the number plate on the bike. It's a false plate. It's one of a batch issued to Royal Mail for their fleet of vans three years ago. It should be a Ford Transit!"

"Not really a surprise, I suppose. Have you put out a stop and detain notice on anyone driving a Honda Pan European with an English plate?"

"Yes, Sarge, and I've alerted the PSNI too, just in case."

"Good. Well done. Do you know how Liam got on with James McGinty? Any sightings or information?"

"No, nothing. He seems to have just vanished. Shall I put out a notice on him too?"

"Yes, OK. But quietly. Nothing public. Just ask the local stations to keep an eye out. We can't arrest him. He's done nothing wrong as far as we know. But it's odd that he's taken off. If anyone finds him, just bring him in to help with enquiries."

"Yes, OK. I'll get on it straight away."

"I think the boss wants us to get together after lunch to compare notes. Anything back from your friend in Sligo on that stuff we collected at the cheese factory?"

"No, Sarge. It would hardly be there yet. Give them a chance."

"I suppose you're right. I'm just feeling impatient. This case is going nowhere. I'm going to pop out for a sandwich. Can I get you anything?"

"No, you're grand, thanks. I'm not hungry."

"OK. See you later then."

"Yes, see ya."

* * *

"OK, everyone, listen up," O'Shea said as he brought the team together after lunch. He went around the group one by one and asked them if there had been any significant developments. When there was nothing new to report, he addressed them himself.

"Right, folks, we don't seem to be getting very far, do we? We need to step this up a gear, start putting a bit of pressure on a few people. I can't help feeling that Conor's research and the college have more to do with it than anything else. Agnes, can you go back over that hard drive we found in the car. Look at everything this time. Documents, spreadsheets, video clips, photographs, emails – the lot. And go back as far as you can. I'm convinced there's something buried deep in there somewhere that's the key to this thing. Liam, will you keep going on McGinty and the motorbike? Deirdre, I'd like you to chase up the lab and see what they can give us. I'm going to continue digging on Pat Nevin and see if I can find anything, anything at all, that could have got him into difficulty. We'll get together again in the morning to compare notes, and if anything breaks, please let me know at once."

Everyone nodded in agreement and went off to complete their assigned tasks.

* * *

Before Maguire left the station, she took a call from her erstwhile boyfriend, Eoin.

"Hi, Deirdre. Sorry to call you at work. But I was wondering if you're free this evening? We could get something to eat in Castlebar if you like?"

"Hi, Eoin. Yes, that would be very nice. What do you fancy?"

"We could try that place you were talking about the other night? What's it called? The Blue something."

"Oh yes, the Blue Serenade. I've heard it's excellent. Why don't you see if you can get us a table for, say, 7:30?"

"Sure! I'll text you a confirmation and pick you up at 7:15 if that's OK?"

"Perfect. Thanks."

Before she got home, she received a text from Eoin telling her that the restaurant was booked for 7:30, and he would collect her at 7:15 as arranged.

He arrived bang on time, and the two of them set off in Eoin's Audi A4. Maguire loved his car. It had pale leather seats and a great heater, as well as full air conditioning. It didn't take them long to get to their destination, and they found parking almost outside the Blue Serenade.

The meal was excellent, as was the service. They both had fillet steaks with French fries and baked root vegetables. The steak was cooked to perfection and melt-in-the-mouth tender.

"This is really good," Maguire said as she sliced another mouthful from the meat.

"Yes, I'm very impressed," Eoin agreed. "Fancy a desert?"

"No, thanks. I'm stuffed. Coffee back at mine?"

Eoin smiled at her and asked for the bill.

Chapter Twenty-Five

He was pleased that it was a dark night on the outskirts of Castlebar. There were heavy grey clouds obscuring the moon high in the sky, but it wasn't actually raining.

As he approached the entrance to the ATU campus, he switched off the lights on the motorbike and coasted to a halt. He'd been past this place a few times in daylight, so he knew there was a good spot to conceal the machine a few hundred yards further on where an old building stood back from the road in a state of ruin. He manoeuvred the heavy bike off the road and into the decrepit place, parked it and fixed a black face mask over his features, leaving his crash helmet in place.

Back down the road a little way, he climbed over the wall at the boundary of the university site and made his way stealthily to the side of the main building. It was 3:30 a.m., and there wasn't a soul about.

The only light that had been left on was over the main door to the building, so the sides of the place were in almost total darkness, which suited his purpose. He approached a long window that was set into the outer wall alongside several others. It reached down to just over a metre short of the grass and was fashioned in what was quite possibly the original wooden frame – which would date back to the nineteenth century. It didn't take him long to slip the catch.

He raised the lower sash gently, waiting for some sort of alarm to go off, but he was met only with silence. As he placed his left leg over the sill to make an entry, he observed a fox standing in the grass looking on curiously at him, but he just smiled and paid no heed.

Once inside, he made his way out of the room he'd entered by into the main hall. Again, no alarm sounded, so using the torch on his mobile phone, he advanced to the stairway and started to climb up.

On the second floor, he soon found the room he was looking for. It wasn't even locked! Inside, the distinctive hum of computer servers filled the thick air, and a wave of heat hit him as he entered. The small amount of light given off by the tower of black servers stacked against the far wall allowed him to move silently in that direction. He took out the heavy, insulated pliers he'd brought with him, located the mains cable going into the server tower and snipped it cleanly. A few sparks fell to the ground, and the characteristic hum faded as each of the machines shut down unexpectedly. After a minute, the room was completely silent.

Using another implement that he removed from inside his leather jacket, the man set about the servers, driving the sharp tool repeatedly into the systems, wrecking their insides. He found the place where the disk storage was located and ripped out seven units from their housing, dropping them on the floor before attacking them with a hammer and smashing them to pieces.

When he'd finished with the servers, he went down along the benches, smashing each of the flat-screen monitors in turn, and pulling them down onto the floor in a tangle of twisted wires and broken glass and plastic.

His final assault was on the filing cabinet located inside the door. He opened it and searched through each of the four drawers. But finding nothing more than hundreds of paper files, he contented himself with removing them and scattering them all over the floor. He contemplated setting fire to all the paper but decided that it might attract too much attention too soon. Even if the university hadn't bothered with a decent burglar alarm, they would be unlikely to have left the place without a fire alarm.

He took a last look around, satisfied with his efforts, and withdrew via the same route as he'd come. The entire operation had taken just nine minutes.

Chapter Twenty-Six

DI Martin O'Shea was sitting at his desk in his office at ten past nine the following morning. Agnes Gallagher and Liam Staunton were at their assigned desks outside in the open-plan area, but there was no sign yet of Deirdre Maguire, which was surprising as she usually beat him to it whenever he had to drop the kids off at school.

The phone on O'Shea's desk rang, and he picked it up. "O'Shea."

"Oh, good morning, sir. I have a Mr Williams on the phone. He asked to speak to Sergeant Maguire, but as she isn't in yet, I wonder would you like to speak to him?"

"Yes, OK. Put him through."

There was a brief musical interlude on the phone, and then Williams came on the line.

"My name is Ellis Williams. Who am I speaking with?" the man said.

"This is Detective Inspector Martin O'Shea. How can I help you, Mr Williams?"

"Good morning, Inspector. I'm the administrator out at the ATU campus in Castlebar. I'm afraid we've had a break-in, and a great deal of damage has been done to our computer suite. It happened during the night. The place is a terrible mess."

"I see. I'm sorry to hear that, Mr Williams, but may I ask why you're calling us? Surely the local uniformed Gardaí in Castlebar should be dealing with this?"

"Well, it's just that Sergeant Maguire was out here with yourself in connection with the death of Conor Nevin. He used the computer facility extensively for his degree program, and I felt that there could be some sort of connection."

"I see. OK, I'll get the local Gardaí to attend as soon as possible. Can you try and ensure that the scene is left undisturbed, Mr Williams? And I'll come out with Sergeant Maguire shortly too."

"Thank you, Inspector. It may not be easy to keep the place isolated. There are lots of students milling around, but I'll do my best till the officers get here. See you soon."

When the call was ended, O'Shea shouted for Agnes Gallagher to come to his office. She appeared in the door a few seconds later.

"Yes, sir. What's up?"

"Look, Agnes, there's been a break-in at the ATU place in Castlebar, and the administrator there thinks there may be a link to the Nevin case. Can you get on to Castlebar Gardaí and get them out there pronto? Ask them to secure the scene and not to muck about with it till we arrive. And where the *hell* is Maguire?"

"Yes, sir. Right away, sir." And with that she left.

O'Shea picked up the phone and dialled Maguire's mobile number. It was answered on the third ring.

"Yes, boss?"

"Where the blazes are you, Deirdre? It's nearly half past nine."

"Good morning to you too, sir. I'm just pulling into

the car park. I'll be with you in a couple of minutes. Where's the fire?"

"Just get in here as soon as you can." He put the phone down rather roughly.

* * *

O'Shea had cooled down a lot by the time they were heading for the ATU campus in Castlebar. Maguire was an outstanding officer, and he had no real reason to be angry with her for being a few minutes late to work when she normally put in all the hours without complaint.

"Do you think there might be a connection to the Nevin case?" O'Shea asked her.

"Well, it's a bit of a coincidence, and neither of us believe in those. It looks to me as if Conor Nevin had discovered something during his research that could be an embarrassment to someone, and they needed to find the material and destroy it."

"Yes, but killing the lad and his father is a bit extreme, don't you think? And this caper looks to be a bit over the top as well. Did you get anything back from Sligo on the inulin sample we got from Westport Way Cheese?"

"No, not yet. I'll follow it up when we get back to the station."

"Yes, OK. I wonder if this latest nonsense is down to the motorbike man as well?"

"Hmm… could be. Tell you what. When we get there, why don't you deal with Williams and the locals, and I'll go for a stroll round and about – see what I can discover?"

"Sounds like a plan. You're on."

* * *

Maguire left her colleague to see to the break-in at the college, walked back to the entrance to the campus on the Westport Road and had a look around. Turning right would lead her up past the hospital and into the centre of town, so she elected to go left, down towards the junction with Lannagh Road.

Before she got to the intersection, there was a narrow lane leading up to the left, and her instincts guided her along the track to where an old derelict shed stood She walked around the old building, and at the side, she found what looked like narrow tyre tracks in the soft earth. She bent down and took a closer look. They were almost certainly left by a motorcycle, so she took out her phone and photographed the impression left by the wheels from as many angles as she could manage, given the rudimentary equipment at her disposal.

Then Maguire walked back onto the Westport Road and up towards the hospital which adjoined the ATU plot. She searched high and low for any CCTV cameras that might have been installed at the entrance to the facility but found none.

Back at the ATU building, officers in white suits were busy brushing grey powder on various window and door frames. The whole area had been taped off, and some small groups of students stood looking on, trying to figure out what all the fuss was about. Maguire found O'Shea talking to Ellis Williams outside on the concrete apron.

"Anything useful, boss?" she asked.

"Not really. Mr Williams here has told me that the building isn't alarmed. They never saw the need, and it's expensive. There's never been a break-in here before, it seems."

"OK. What about inside? Has anything obvious been stolen?"

"No, but whoever it was made a right mess of the computer laboratory," O'Shea said.

Then Williams spoke up. "Yes, there's tens of thousands of euro worth of damage. It's a real disaster. And it'll take us ages to get all that stuff replaced and up and running. The students will be very seriously disadvantaged," he said grimly.

"Oh, I don't know, Mr Williams. Who supplied your IT equipment?" O'Shea asked.

"It's all Dell. They're very good to us."

"Yes, and to be fair, I think this is just the kind of situation where they'd be delighted to get stuck in and get you up and running as soon as possible. They get great PR from this sort of thing. So, as soon as our lot have finished, you should get on to them and see what they can do. I'd say they'd have you up and running in less than a week."

"Do you really think so, Inspector? I must go and talk to Professor Mulligan at once. He's our head of IT. I'll tell him what you said."

When Williams had gone off to find the professor, Maguire told O'Shea about the motorbike tracks.

"Good work, Deirdre. Get forensics onto it as soon as. Any sign of CCTV anywhere about?"

"No, 'fraid not. There's probably something up at the hospital, but not near the gate. And if he came in from the Lannagh Road end, then we're stuffed."

"OK, but there must be some cameras somewhere in the town. Ask the local boys to see if they can dig up anything."

"Right. What's the story inside?" Maguire asked.

"It's a right old mess. Looks like chummy attacked all the IT servers and destroyed the hard drives. I'm not sure if they have backups, but it was a fairly serious attempt to eliminate something, that's for sure.

Chapter Twenty-Seven

Shane Nevin was fuming as only teenagers can.

He was livid. Some bastard had come into their relatively peaceful lives, and screwed them over by killing his dad and his brother. Shane's own life would now take a different course than the one he'd envisaged. Things would never be the same again. His poor mother was destroyed. How could she possibly cope with such a tragedy? It wasn't fair. And the Gardaí hadn't a clue. As far as he was concerned, they just drove around from one coffee shop to another making jokes and laughing at ordinary people. It meant nothing to them that his and his mother's lives had changed so dramatically in the wink of an eye, and they had no idea of a motive. Fat lot of good they were. No. If there was to be justice in this case, Shane himself would have to find it. Somehow, he would locate the bastard that had done this to them and sort him out.

It wouldn't be nice. He'd make sure the fucker knew how much he'd hurt them. Shane imagined a slow and very painful death for the killer at his hands. He would scream for mercy, but none would be given. He would writhe in agony as Shane cut him here and there about his body. As his lifeblood leaked out, he would slowly lose consciousness, but Shane would bring him around by splashing his face with icy-cold, salted water, just to sting his many wounds a bit more, and he would continue for many hours, perhaps even days, till life left the bugger for good. Better than a few years in a cushy cell in Mountjoy Prison watching daytime TV, that was for sure.

Shane went over and over this scenario in his head as he went about his now daily task of trying to manage the farm. He let his imagination loose, and with every visit to that dark place, the treatment the killer would receive got worse. These thoughts intruded on his everyday life, and at night they blossomed, sending him off to a restless sleep to dream some more about what lay in store for his victim.

Shane was out walking the fields that afternoon trying to clear his head. It was something his father had taught him. Whenever a knotty problem was troubling Pat Nevin, he would spend a few hours outdoors, just ambling around his acreage, perhaps talking briefly to some of his cattle, and generally taking the clean country air. Somehow, after a few hours of aimless meandering, things would resolve themselves in his head, and he could get on with whatever had been bothering him, and Shane was now doing the same, hoping for a similar effect.

As he strolled along beside the stream that ran between the lower half-acre, as they called it, and the road, he glanced down onto the bank above the water which flowed freely over the pebbles and stones in the stream bed, making soothing rippling noises. The sun caught on something shiny lodged against the bank, largely concealed under the weedy overhang, and reflected a shaft of light up into Shane's eyes.

Curious, Shane eased himself down into the shallow stream, thankful that he'd put on wellington boots for his outing, and retrieved the object that had caught his attention.

"Well, well, what have we here?" he said, smiling to himself. "I knew that lot were bloody useless! This is probably the knife that was used to kill Dad and Conor."

Shane was holding the weapon carefully between his first finger and thumb just where the handle joined the blade so as not to contaminate the item. But his mind was racing. Should he contact the Gardaí? No, he thought. Better to keep the knife. When he caught up with the blaggard that had used it on his family, it would be a nice irony for him to wield it in revenge. It would make retribution all the sweeter.

Shane made his way back to the barn that housed his quad bike and all the tools used on the farm. He went inside and found a piece of old sackcloth. He carefully wrapped the knife in the dusty cloth and stashed it at the back of an old metal toolbox under the workbench. He placed the toolbox back carefully so that the knife couldn't be seen, and no disturbance could be observed – not that it was likely anyone would be looking.

His next mission was to locate the perpetrator. He knew that a motorbike had been used as transport for the villain, but whether or not he was still in the vicinity, he didn't know. But Shane figured that it was unlikely to be a local person that had done the dreaded deed, so how hard could it be to find some out-of-towner with a motorbike at this time of year? He figured it hadn't occurred to the dumb cops to follow that line of enquiry, so he would get busy.

Sitting in his bedroom later that evening, a notebook open on his small desk, he started to make a list. First, he would check out the hotels and B&Bs in the town to see if a guest with a motorbike had been staying in any of them, then he'd check out the petrol stations in the area. There weren't many. A number had closed over the last few years, and those that remained were quite extensive, incorporating a decent-sized shop, a fuel store, and several petrol and diesel pumps as well as a service area for air and water, and even a huge car wash. Shane figured that most of these places would have CCTV to record motorists filling their tanks in case any should decide to make off without paying. So he needed to get access to the footage to see if a motorbike had stopped for a refill at any of them. He wasn't sure quite how to go about this, but he'd think of something.

Chapter Twenty-Eight

When Deirdre Maguire got to the Garda station the following morning, there was a file on her desk that had come in from the pharmaceutical lab in Sligo. She took off her jacket and hung it on the back of her chair, then sat down to read the report.

What she discovered surprised her greatly. A detailed analysis of the inulin she'd collected from Westport Way Cheese had been carried out, and the conclusion was that the substance was impure. Very impure. It had apparently been cut with a large number of microplastic granules. This stuff would be a lot cheaper than the natural ingredients inulin was made from but could be damaging to people who ingested it.

The report cited various academic papers on the subject, and Maguire took a few minutes to look up a few of them and scan quickly through the abstracts. Much of the research was inconclusive, but this was more to do with lack of relevant investigation rather than giving MPs, as they were referred to, a clean bill of health.

Maguire finished the report and closed the file. She needed to bring the DI up to date with this new information, and she envisaged a trip to Mrs Blenerhassett at the Westport Way Cheese factory. Could this somehow have provided the motive for the death of Conor Nevin and his father?

O'Shea was in his office when Maguire marched in with the forensic report under her arm.

"What have you got there, Deirdre?" O'Shea asked.

"It's the forensic report on that stuff I collected from the cheese factory. It's not nice."

"Oh? Do tell."

Maguire summarized the report for her boss, who absorbed the information quietly as she was speaking.

"Hmm… And you're thinking this could be connected to the two murders? Just help me out here. Join the dots for me," O'Shea said.

"Well, let's say Conor, who was into microbiology as part of his degree, somehow discovered the information about the inulin. He prints out all the supporting papers on the matter, and he goes across to the ATU campus during the night to collect all the data with his dad. Someone who has a keen interest in this information not getting out decides to relieve Conor of the research and silence him at the same time. The father was just collateral damage."

"Yes, but why go to the campus in the middle of the night? He could have just brought it home with him after college one day," O'Shea said.

"I don't know. Maybe he was threatened or something. That bit does seem slightly odd. But it would explain why the IT at the college was thrashed too. Whoever's behind this obviously thought all his stuff would be on the servers."

"OK. You may be right, but it's not going to be easy to flush all that out. I suppose we'd better start with the cheese lady. Can you go out and see her? Take Liam or Agnes with you and give her a good rattle. Bring her in if you have to."

"OK. What are you going to do, boss?"

"I'm going to take this upstairs. Superintendent O'Connell may have to get the Food Safety Authority involved. But we can't get distracted. We have a double murder to solve."

"Right. Let's keep in touch."

Maguire took Agnes Gallagher with her for her visit to Westport Way Cheese. They found Mrs Blenerhassett all decked out in a white coat and blue hair covering in the cheese plant. As they approached her, she said, "Sorry, Sergeant, you're not allowed in here without protective clothing. We can talk outside."

The two Gardaí went back outside and waited for Blenerhassett to join them.

"So what can I do for you today, ladies?" Blenerhassett asked.

"You may recall, Mrs Blenerhassett, when I was last here, I took a sample of that inulin stuff away with me," Maguire said.

"Yes, I remember. So what?"

"We had that sample analysed, and it was found to contain a significant amount of microplastics. The inulin isn't anything like pure, and not to put a tooth in it, it could well be poisoning your customers."

"That's nonsense, Sergeant! We've never had any complaints about our products. Not even one."

"That doesn't surprise me, Mrs Blenerhassett. Your customers wouldn't even be aware of the impurity. But it could be affecting their internal organs without them being aware."

"Look, Sergeant, are you sure about this? I mean, it all seems a bit far-fetched to me. We've been using inulin for years, and surely we would have found out if there was an issue."

"I can't comment on that, Mrs Blenerhassett, but I can give you a copy of the lab report if you wish, and of course, you can have your own analysis carried out too. But for now, there are some precautions you need to take."

"Such as?" the woman asked, clearly getting quite rattled by what Maguire was telling her.

"I think it would be wise if you stopped putting inulin into the cheese at once. You may have to recall all the product that's out for sale too, but that's down to the Food Safety Authority. We have notified them. And I need full details of where you bought the inulin of course."

"I can't do that. It will destroy us. I've spent years building up my brand. If I have to recall the cheese, my customers will never trust us again."

Maguire was starting to feel a little impatient with her. "Mrs Blenerhassett, I can't stand here all day arguing with you. Can you please go inside and get the supplier information for us and give it to Agnes here? I need to call my DI."

Gallagher went off with a very grumpy Mrs Blenerhassett, while Maguire placed a call to O'Shea.

"Hi, boss. What's the story?"

"Hi, Deirdre. I've spoken to the boss. He's called the FSA and advised them, and they're sending down an inspector from Dublin tomorrow. Can you make sure they don't deliver any more product today and see if you can secure the stock of inulin somehow?"

"OK. I'll see what I can do, but Blenerhassett isn't convinced and is very worried about their reputation. No surprise really. This could damage them quite badly."

"Yes, I know. But that's not really our concern. You need to find out where she bought this stuff and get tracking the supplier. If you're right, this could well be connected to the Nevins' killings."

"OK, boss. I'll stay on it here till we get a result, and then I'll be back in. See you in a while."

Chapter Twenty-Nine

Detective Garda Agnes Gallagher lived with her parents in a modest but well cared for semi-detached house on the southern outskirts of Castlebar in an area known as The Curragh. Her two brothers, with whom she'd grown up, had flown the nest some time ago. Her eldest brother, Anthony, worked for a big insurance company in Norwich in the UK, while her younger brother, Brian, had a driving school in the suburbs of Dublin. Brian had been car mad since he was a small child and had found the driving school a good way to exploit his passion whilst earning a living at the same time.

Agnes's parents were in their early sixties. Her father ran a large hardware and electrical shop in Castlebar, while her mother worked part-time in the same business, keeping the books and accounts.

Agnes had her bedroom at the front of the house, overlooking the front garden and the road. She kept the room very tidy, as was her nature, and she helped her mother extensively in the house, spending much of her free time assisting with the cleaning and the cooking.

She was sound asleep in her cosy double bed when her slumber was disturbed by a noise downstairs. She looked at the radio alarm clock on the nightstand and saw that it was just coming up to 6 a.m. She turned over, believing that she could get back to sleep easily, when she heard it again. There was definitely something going on that wasn't normal. Both of her parents were sound sleepers and never got up this early.

Agnes was now more awake. She listened intently for any repeat of the sound that had woken her but could hear nothing. Nevertheless, she decided to get up and make sure that there was no one in the house. She stepped out of bed, donned her dressing gown – which had been hanging on a hook on the back of the door – and, keeping as silent as she could manage, gently opened her bedroom door.

As soon as the door was opened a little, a figure dressed all in black with a balaclava over its head barged into her room, brandishing a knife. The intruder quickly put his hand over Agnes's mouth and whispered to her to stay quiet or he would stab her.

Agnes was pushed back onto the bed, and the intruder stood in front of her with his menacing-looking blade extended towards her upper torso.

"Now, missy," he said in a gravelly voice, "this is what happens next. I'm going to stay here to look after Mum and Dad, while you go into the cop shop and retrieve Conor Nevin's laptop and bring it here to me. If you do that without causing any fuss or alerting anyone about me, your folks will be quite safe, I'll disappear with the computer and you'll never see me again. But if anything goes wrong – well, you know. Got it?"

Agnes nodded. She was thinking quickly, even in her sleepy state. Could she overpower her assailant? Once outside the house, could she call in the cavalry, or would this guy attack her parents just for spite? She quickly made up her mind to do what was asked, and not to take a chance with the lives of her mother and father.

"I can't go into the Garda station until about eight o'clock. It would look very suspicious. But I'll do as you say, as long as you promise not to hurt my parents."

"OK. Well, why don't we go downstairs and have a nice cup of tea till it's time for you to go?"

Agnes was thinking quickly. "You'll have to leave the room while I get dressed," she said.

"Ha ha. Very good. No chance. I'll look away while you change. Don't worry – I'm no pervert."

As she shed her night clothes and donned her daytime wear, she tried to think if she'd heard that voice previously. And where was his accent from? It wasn't local, that was for sure.

The man did as he said he would, and a few minutes later, Agnes was fully dressed in her work clothes.

"Right. Let's go," she said to the man, who ushered her out of the room ahead of him. They were downstairs in the kitchen when Mrs Gallagher arrived in her own dressing gown to start preparing breakfast for herself and her husband.

"What's going on?" she exclaimed when she saw the uninvited guest.

The man grabbed the woman and pushed her roughly down into one of the kitchen chairs. He then took a roll of duct tape from his pocket and proceeded to secure Mrs Gallagher to the chair.

"Don't be rough with her. You said you wouldn't harm her," Agnes exclaimed.

"She'll be fine. But I can't take a chance on her doing

something daft. Now off you go, Agnes, and get me the laptop. The sooner you're back, the sooner I'll be gone."

Agnes left the house and set off in her car for Westport Garda station. She was very conflicted. Should she tell Maguire what was going on, or should she just do as the man had asked and hope that he wouldn't hurt her parents? As she drove along, she tried to rationalize the situation and decide what to do.

She was the first of the team to arrive at the station. Before any of the others appeared, she went to the evidence store and quickly located Conor Nevin's laptop. She tucked it under her jacket and, feeling much like a thief herself, managed to get back out to her car without anyone other than the desk sergeant, who seemed totally disinterested, seeing her.

* * *

Soon after Agnes had left her home, Mr Gallagher came downstairs, having washed and shaved in preparation for the day ahead. As he descended the last few steps of the carpeted staircase, he could hear a conversation going on in the kitchen. His wife was saying to someone, "You'll never get away with this," to which a rough male voice responded, "Shut up. If your daughter has any sense, she'll do as I say and I'll be gone in another half hour. So pipe down and stay quiet."

On hearing this, Mr Gallagher retreated upstairs as silently as he could. He was grateful that the stairs didn't creak, and he made it back to the shelter of their double bedroom without being detected. He quickly found his mobile phone and called Agnes.

"What's going on, Agnes? There's someone downstairs with your mother."

"I know, Dad. Don't worry. It's all fine. I'm on my way back to the house. Where are you?"

"I'm upstairs in the bedroom. What's this all about?"

Agnes told her father about their visitor's demands and tried to reassure him that she had everything under control.

"I can't just do nothing," he replied. "What if he decides to use the knife on your mam? Is this the same bloke that stabbed the Nevins?"

"I don't know. It could be. But please, leave it alone. I'm only a few minutes away, and if he gets what I have here for him, he'll probably just leave. He has no reason to hurt any of us."

"OK. But hurry up. I'm not a bit happy with this arrangement," Mr Gallagher said.

When Agnes had finished the call, her father made a decision. He used his smartphone to locate the telephone number of Westport Garda station, called the number and asked to be put through to DI O'Shea.

Chapter Thirty

O'Shea had just arrived at work when he took the call from Gallagher. "Hello, Mr Gallagher. I understand you're Agnes's father, is that right?"

"Yes, Inspector. And I'm calling from my bedroom. There's a man downstairs in our house holding my wife at knifepoint. He's forced Agnes to go into the station and collect Conor Nevin's computer. Agnes is on her way back now."

"Has you wife been hurt, Mr Gallagher?"

"No, I don't think so, but obviously I'm very concerned that he might hurt her. This may be the same man that killed the Nevins."

"OK. Well, it might be best if you stayed out of the way for now. I'll get things moving from here. Can you just confirm your address for me?"

Gallagher reeled off the address, and O'Shea ended the call.

O'Shea didn't want to endanger Agnes Gallagher's parents, so he decided to put a plan into action that would, in his view, be safe but would still allow them to apprehend the villain. He launched Google Maps on his office PC and entered the address Gallagher had given him. He then called Castlebar Garda station, explained the situation to a DI he knew there and asked how many cars they could deploy to intercept their target, given that he would, in all probability, be riding a powerful motorbike.

His colleague said they could probably get four cars out at short notice, and O'Shea arranged for them to be positioned at two different locations on Humbert Way. There wasn't time to arrange for an armed response unit, so the men in the Garda cars would have to use their initiative to stop and detain the rider – and hopefully recover the laptop.

* * *

Agnes arrived back at her house, got out of her car and went directly to the kitchen, where her mother was still tethered to the chair. The masked intruder was sitting quite calmly in another kitchen chair.

When Agnes came in, the man stood up. "Did you get it?"

"Yes, I have it here. But I'm only going to give it to you outside the house. I want you out of here."

The man stared at Agnes intently through the holes in his mask for what seemed like an age. Eventually, he waved the knife towards the door, and Agnes led the two of them outside. Standing on her driveway, she handed over the laptop, which the man put inside his jacket. He then went around the side of the house and mounted his Honda, started it and took off at high speed.

Agnes rushed into the house to see to her mother. Her father arrived down too, and both of them started fussing over Mrs Gallagher, who was now liberated from her chair and rubbing her rather red wrists where the tape had been.

"Has he gone?" Mr Gallagher asked.

"Yes. He's got what he wanted. Thank God he didn't hurt you, Mam. Are you OK?"

"Yes, yes, I'm fine. Don't fuss. What about you? Are you OK?"

"Yes. I'm a bit shook up. I'm not used to having masked intruders in my bedroom, but he didn't do anything to me," Agnes replied, keen to reassure her parents that she hadn't be molested.

"He won't get far anyway. While you were off out, I called your boss in Westport, and he's set up road blocks out on Humbert Way. They probably have him by now."

* * *

But that wasn't the case.

The biker had gone back through the housing estate, but when he saw the Garda cars lined up at the exit of the estate, he turned around. He drove back the way he'd come, turned onto Aglish, followed the road around to the left, flew through a gap in the fence into the grounds of the Corrib Oil petrol station and took off. The Gardaí manning the roadblocks saw him departing, but by the time they'd turned their vehicles around and were ready to give chase, he was long gone.

* * *

Agnes's phone rang.

"Agnes. This is DI O'Shea. Are you all OK?"

"Yes, thanks, sir. Yer man is away off with Nevin's laptop, but it won't do him any good."

"How's that?" O'Shea asked.

"When that thing came in, the first thing I did was to make a clone copy of the hard drive, remember? And before I handed it over to him, I stopped on the way home and deleted the entire system. What he's got is useless."

"Christ, Agnes, that was taking a chance. What if he'd powered it up at your house?"

"I couldn't just hand over the thing, sir. It wouldn't have been right."

"OK. Well, well done, you. I have the lads in Castlebar on his trail now. Apparently, he gave them the slip, but I can't see him getting too far."

"Right. Will I come into work now, sir?"

"Yes, if you're feeling up to it. I'll get Castlebar to post a uniformed officer outside your house for the rest of the day, and overnight tonight too, in case he comes back."

"Thanks, sir. I'll see you soon."

Chapter Thirty-One

Shane Nevin had been busy. Using both his father's jeep and his quad bike for transport, he'd travelled around large areas of Westport and Castlebar trying to locate the mysterious motorbike rider. As planned, he started with the petrol stations. He spun them a yarn that the motorbike was his and had been stolen, which earned him the sympathy of the cashiers, who allowed him to scan their CCTV.

On his third stop, he struck it lucky. He could see the biker arriving at the pumps, filling up his Honda and then coming in to pay. The petrol station had a camera focused on the hatch where money was given in, and the killer's face could clearly be seen as he handed over payment for the petrol. He also bought a wrapped sandwich and two bars of chocolate, and paid for it all with a €50 note.

Shane persuaded the cashier to let him take a few photos of the CCTV with his phone, and when he left, he had three fairly clear images of his quarry.

When he'd secured the images, he went back home and printed them off on his inkjet printer. They weren't great, but he figured they could be helpful if he had to ask people if they'd seen the man recently.

He had to slot his sleuthing in between managing the farm. Séan Lynch, the neighbouring farmer, had agreed to take the livestock, but he wanted a couple of weeks to get their pasture organized. It had been lying fallow, and though it had a good covering of sweet grass and clover, the fences weren't completely secure. He'd asked Shane to help him install an electric fence around the perimeter of the field in which the cattle would graze, and this had activity prevented Shane from applying himself full-time to detecting. But he wasn't put off.

He scoured Airbnb and Google for all the holiday lets and guest houses in the area that might have appealed to his target, but it was a daunting task. There were literally hundreds of locations, and there was some possibility, however remote, that the biker could even be holed up in a tent in some out-of-the-way place where he'd never be found.

But Shane Nevin was determined to get revenge for the killing of his brother and father, and no amount of work would distract him from that goal. In fact, as he toiled away in the fields, he thought of little else. And in an odd way, this made him even more determined to get justice for his father and his elder brother.

So every day, once all the other things he had to do were out of the way, he turned his attention to his quest. He stayed up long into the night researching, and sometimes he even went out after dark to investigate a location to see if there was a motorbike parked nearby, but so far, he hadn't found anything.

* * *

Despite their best efforts, the Castlebar Gardaí had been unable to trace the person on the motorbike. It was like he'd just vanished into thin air. There were no road cameras installed in the area, so they were relying on their pursuit of the escaping biker, which had led them exactly nowhere.

Back in Westport, the detectives were huddled together trying to figure out their next move and assess where the investigation was at.

"OK, folks. Let's summarize exactly where we are," DI O'Shea said to the little group.

Agnes Gallagher was first to speak. "Well, sir, he may have got Conor Nevin's laptop, but it's not going to do him any good. As I said, I managed to wipe it before I handed it over, and everything was on that separate hard drive we found and cloned anyway. They obviously didn't know about that."

"That's great, Agnes. We need to do more with that. There must be something on it that can explain what all this is about. Can you keep working on the hard drive?"

"Yes, sir, I'll get onto it right away. I'll check in with forensics on the phone they collected from the scene too – see if they've been able to get anything else from it.

"Right, thanks. How are you feeling, by the way?" O'Shea said.

"I'm fine, thank you, sir. I just want to keep busy."

"Great. Now, Deirdre, what's happening with this inulin stuff from the cheese factory?"

"We've told Blenerhassett not to send out any more product, and we've secured the bags of the stuff she has out at the plant. She gave me a dose of paperwork relating to the supply of the inulin too, and I'm about to start tracing it back to source. What's happening with the Food Safety crowd?" Maguire asked.

"They're sending an inspector down today. I think we'll let them deal with that aspect of things. We have enough to be doing. Is there anything back from forensics about the break-in at the college?" O'Shea asked.

"We need to follow that up too, sir," Maguire replied.

"Yes. Can you get on that too?"

"Maybe Liam could get on to that, sir. I'll be kind of busy."

"Yes, OK. Are you up for it, Liam?"

Staunton said that he was, and that he would talk to Maguire after the meeting to get the details.

"Right. It looks as if we've a lot to be getting on with. Let's meet back at five o'clock for an update, and as usual, if anything breaks, keep me informed."

They all nodded their agreement and went off to see to their various tasks.

Chapter Thirty-Two

The man sat on the grass beside his Honda, which was cooling down, its engine making ticking noises as the metal contracted. He had Conor Nevin's laptop on the ground beside him, but he hadn't attempted to turn it on. He had, after all, only been asked to get it, not look at the content.

He took out his mobile phone and dialled the only number that was in the memory of the device.

"Yes," the person at the other end growled.

"OK. I've got the laptop, as you asked. I've done everything you wanted. Now I need my money."

"Your money will be in the locker that we agreed later on today. I suggest you disappear as soon as you have it."

"Don't worry – I'm not hanging around. What about the laptop?"

"Destroy it. And do a decent job. We don't want anyone getting into it. Clear?"

"Yes. And the bike?"

"Dump it in the sea, and don't get seen. And don't call this number again."

The line went dead.

He looked at the computer he'd taken from Agnes Gallagher. It was almost new. He didn't know much about these things, but he recognized the branding. It was a Lenovo X1, and it looked expensive. Maybe he could get an extra few hundred if he sold it on. After all, why destroy a perfectly good computer? The man would never know.

And he was getting quite fond of the Honda Pan European too. It had proven its worth when he'd had to evade the police after he left Agnes Gallagher's place. It was fast, smooth, quiet and stuck to the road like chewing gum. OK, so it was stolen, but he could sort that out once he got back to England. He'd get new papers for it as a Japanese import and get it registered, and no one would be any the wiser.

He stroked the bike affectionately as he got up from his sitting position. "Don't worry – I'll not be dumping you in the sea, old friend."

Chapter Thirty-Three

Deirdre Maguire was starting to explore the sheaf of documentation Mrs Blenerhassett had given them relating to the inulin. It was anything but straightforward. With her computer at the ready on the Google search page, she picked up the first invoice.

The product had been supplied by a company in the Netherlands. Blenerhassett had been charged €425 plus shipping for each 40 kg bag of inulin, and there were five bags in each consignment. The paperwork went back over two years, during which time the inulin had increased in price from €295 a bag to the current price.

Digging a little deeper, Maguire discovered that the supplement was actually manufactured in China. This was substantiated by writing on the outside of the bag of inulin that the Gardaí had brought back from the factory. A company called Chi-Supp were the manufacturers, and writing on the bag, which was in several languages – fortunately including English – described the content as "Pure fructans extracted from organic vegetable matter, including chicory. Certified food safe under licence number CH344908-077."

Maguire googled Chi-Supp, but unfortunately the firm's website appeared to be in Chinese, which, of course, Maguire couldn't read. But it didn't matter really. It looked as if the product had been packed in China, and had simply been warehoused and sold on by the firm in the Netherlands.

Maguire noted the phone number on the invoices Blenerhassett had provided and called it. Fortunately, people in the Netherlands spent at least six years in school learning English, so she had no difficulty in communicating with them. After a little bit of to and fro, she got through to a man called Hendrik Blaat, who was, apparently, the export sales manager.

"Good day, Mr Blaat. My name is Detective Sergeant Deirdre Maguire from the police in Ireland. I'm making enquiries about a food supplement that you sold to a company here called Westport Way Cheese. The product is inulin, and it comes from a Chinese company called Chi-Supp. Are you familiar with this transaction, sir?"

"Let me see. I'll have to look up our system. One moment please."

Maguire could hear Blaat tapping his computer keyboard, and after a few moments, he said, "Ah, yes. I see it. Yes, we've supplied a number of consignments of inulin to that company. And they pay us by bank transfer. It's all in order. May I ask why you have an interest, Sergeant?"

"Mr Blaat, we've had this product forensically analysed in a laboratory here, and we've discovered that it's not pure, as stated on the packaging, but is in fact mixed with quite a high percentage of microplastics. As such, it couldn't be certified as 'food safe'. Do you know anything about this?"

"No. Of course not. Are you sure your analysis is correct?" Blaat asked.

"Yes, I am. And I'm afraid there's more to the story. The person who discovered this was a college student here, studying microbiology as part of his agricultural science degree, and unfortunately, he's been murdered. It seems there may be a connection between his death and his findings."

"Good God. This is unbelievable. We've had no problems with this product or the supplier, and we've been using them for some years. We get other supplements from Chi-Supp as well."

"May I ask if you've ever had reason to analyse any of these products to see that the contents of the packages are what they say they are?"

"No, of course not. I should say that we're just a wholesaler. We have a product list of some 2,000 lines. We can't analyse them all, Sergeant."

"Of course not, but I hope you would agree that you have some responsibility to ensure that what you're selling is what it says on the packaging. Anyway, that's not my concern. The Irish Food Safety Authority will be in touch with you about this, and I can't say that they won't want to bring a prosecution. I suggest you block any further sales of the inulin from this source until they've spoken to you."

"I see. Well, of course we always have the best interests of our customers in mind, but I think this is very unusual."

"Can you give me a contact for Chi-Supp? Preferably someone who speaks English."

"I'll have to get back to you on that, Sergeant. Give me your details."

Maguire called out her phone number and email address. "Maybe you could get back to me today, Mr Blaat? Oh, and I'd like to know the total value of the transactions that your company has with Chi-Supp on an annual basis too."

"I don't know. That's commercially sensitive information, Sergeant. I can't divulge that."

"Very well. In that case, I shall have to get in touch with the Dutch police and ask them to investigate on our behalf. This is a serious matter. Two people have died in connection with this, and one of my officers has been seriously assaulted. This doesn't stop here."

"Very well, Sergeant. I think we're don.," And the line went dead.

Maguire held the telephone out in front of her and shrugged. "Hmph. Nice," she said to herself.

Maguire was pleased that she'd made the call on the Garda station landline. It would have been recorded, and she could get a transcript of the call printed out and pass it on to the FSA inspector.

The call also underscored Maguire's growing uneasiness that the death of Conor Nevin, and his father, was directly connected to the contaminated supplement. She went to find DI O'Shea.

Chapter Thirty-Four

Agnes Gallagher contacted the forensic team. "Hi, it's Agnes Gallagher here. Who's that?"

"It's Kevin here, Agnes. What's up?"

"Hi, Kevin. I'm looking for any more information you might have recovered from the phone that was found out at the Nevins' farm the night they were killed."

"Oh, OK. Give me a minute. I think it's been written up. Ah, yes, here it is. Now, let's see. Yeah, we finally got the backups loaded, and there's some interesting exchanges on WhatsApp."

"OK. Any chance you could print it all out and send it over? I don't want to go through it on the phone."

"Yes, sure. I'll email it. You should have it in a few minutes. I heard you had a bit of a nasty time at your house, Agnes. Are you OK?"

"Oh, that. Yeah. It was a bit terrifying at the time, but I'm fine now. The sarge has the house protected now in case the dude comes back, but I don't think he will. He got what he came for – Conor Nevin's laptop."

"Shit. Was there much stuff on it?"

"No. Nothing. I managed to wipe it before I handed it over, and he was using a separate hard drive they didn't know about anyway," Gallagher said.

"Nice one. You should be working with us. You're wasted as a detective."

"Thanks very much, but I don't think so. Oh, great. Your email has just arrived."

"No problem. You're welcome. Enjoy!"

Gallagher opened the email. It had a PDF attachment, which she saved to her hard drive then opened. There were 15 pages of conversations that had been recovered from Conor Nevin's phone, and they made for very interesting reading.

Walsh had obligingly organized the various exchanges into groups. The first group was between Conor and Maeve Kilcoyne, and it was clear that they'd been quite close. There was nothing salacious in the messages, but there was a lot of warmth and kindness exchanged between them, and it was clear that they cared a lot for each other. Gallagher wondered why Maeve Kilcoyne had been less than honest about her relationship with Conor. They were much closer than she'd implied under interview, but maybe her mother didn't approve for some reason.

The next group of messages were between Conor and James McGinty. These were terse, and not very nice. They referred to Conor's relationship with Maeve Kilcoyne and were a crude attempt to warn Conor off. Conor's replies were quite understated. There was no evidence that either McGinty or Nevin had been anything other than verbal with each other.

There were also a few messages between Conor and Adam Wallace, but these were trivial, just arranging meetings in town and so on.

The last group of WhatsApp messages were more relevant. These were between Conor and someone called

Fu Li Chung. The number was one that Gallagher didn't recognize. It started with +8621, but that didn't help her much. The exchanges were brief, but it was clear that Conor had been demanding money from Chung in exchange for his silence. He'd briefly outlined what he'd discovered about the inulin product, and how he had documentary evidence which he might make public, which would have a detrimental effect on Chung's business. He was demanding €20,000.

Chung had asked Conor for details of his discovery, and Conor had, perhaps foolishly, revealed that he was a microbiology student at ATU in Mayo.

Gallagher couldn't quite believe what she was reading. This was dynamite. It provided a motive, however unlikely, for the demise of Conor Nevin. But who exactly Fu Li Chung was she knew not at this stage – or how he might have been able to arrange to silence Conor Nevin and his father.

Gallagher printed off the PDF file and put a large foldback clip around the top of the pages. She then went in search of Deirdre Maguire.

* * *

"Crikey, Agnes. Bloody hell! We need to find out who this Chung person is and how he fits into this puzzle. Do some research on the web and see if you can find out anything. I'm going to find the DI and bring him up to speed. Well done," Maguire said.

When Maguire had departed, Gallagher set about the internet to see if she could track down this Fu Li Chung. She had a phone number, but that wasn't much help. To her dismay, when she put the name into Google, there were over four million results. She looked at the first twenty or so but could see no connection to their case at all. She then tried LinkedIn, X, Instagram and even TikTok but still could make no connection to the production of food supplements or anything remotely like it.

More from despair than hope, she took a burner mobile phone that the Gardaí kept for times when they wanted to remain anonymous and sent a very brief WhatsApp message to the number she'd recovered from Conor's phone. It simply said, "Call me." She waited patiently for the message to travel to wherever Chung was located. One small grey tick mark appeared at the foot of the message, but that only indicated that the message had been sent. She waited a few more minutes, but the second tick mark that would signify that the message had reached its destination didn't appear.

"Damn," she said in frustration and threw the phone back into the desk drawer.

Chapter Thirty-Five

Shane Nevin had been busy. He'd taken the day off school and gone to every B & B establishment he could find in Westport, and even into Castlebar, enquiring about a visitor with a large Honda motorbike, but had drawn a blank.

He'd then repeated the investigation at the various hotels in the area with the same result. Next up would be the Airbnb sites, of which there were quite a few. But he would have to leave that for another day.

It was late at night when Shane was out on his quadbike, touring around the outskirts of Westport, looking in the various small wooded areas along the banks of the Carrowbeg River that meandered from Kinlooey Lough to the Atlantic Ocean. He was driving through the grounds of Westport House when he thought he saw a thin plume of smoke rising from amongst the densely packed trees on a section of elevated ground backlit by the moon.

Shane stopped the vehicle and dismounted. He went to the back of the quad bike, where there was a large plastic storage bin fixed to the machine, opened it and took out the long-bladed knife that he'd recovered from the stream on his father's land. Moving stealthily, he made his way silently in the direction of the smoke, stopping every few paces to ensure that there was no sudden movement in the undergrowth anywhere near him.

He moved quietly along, sheltering behind the trees as he drew closer to where he thought the man might be hiding. As he approached, he could hear the crackling of a wood fire, and he soon spotted the Honda leaning up against a tree. There was a small one-man tent pitched in a tiny clearing between the trees, and sticking out through the opening, facing the glowing flames, he could see the closed end of a sleeping bag, which was clearly occupied.

Shane raised the knife to waist height and ran his thumb across the blade, savouring the sharpness of the implement. This was what he'd been waiting for. It was his chance to avenge the brutal deaths of his father and brother. He had no doubt that this was the man who'd so callously stabbed them both in cold blood. Shane would make him pay with his own life.

As he stood there, once more contemplating how exactly he would use the blade to make the killer suffer, his thoughts began to change. Despite his desperate quest for revenge, his original plan to draw the killer's death out, he thought about the consequences of what he was about to do. He had little doubt that the Gardaí would connect him to the murder of this despicable specimen, and then he'd probably be given a life sentence, in spite of the injustice. He thought of his mother, who would be left totally on her own, unable to manage the farm single-handedly, and would be completely destroyed by the loss of her remaining son. Things were bad enough for her as it was, but at least she had him, and he was providing great support for her at the moment.

He was sorely conflicted, but as these thoughts began to overtake his bloodlust, he slowly put the knife down by his side. Tears formed in his eyes and ran freely down his cheeks. What to do? Should he complete the task he'd been so intent on for the past few days? Or should he leave it? Should he call the Gardaí and give them the location of the campsite, and let their kind of justice sort it out? A maelstrom of thoughts tumbled through his head.

* * *

The night man in Westport Garda station was enjoying a bit of peace. He'd just made himself a mug of tea, and he was settling down to watch the small portable television that was installed underneath the front desk. Things had been very quiet, as usual at this time of night.

When the telephone rang, interrupting his peace, he answered it with a light sigh. "Westport Gardaí."

"Hello. This is Shane Nevin. I'm out in the grounds of Westport House, and I've found the killer."

"Hold on a second now, son. What killer would that be?" the sergeant asked, thinking he might have a crank on the line.

"The man who killed my brother and father of course. He's camped out here in a small copse. I think he's asleep."

"And where exactly are you?"

"I'm here too. But he can't see me or hear me. I'm down on the path now," Shane said.

"OK. Well, Shane, stay where you are. I'll get someone out to you as soon as we can. Don't go near him. We'll deal with it."

The night man called DI O'Shea when Shane had gone off the line. O'Shea thanked the man for his call, despite the unsociable hour, and said he and Maguire would deal with it immediately.

* * *

An hour later, O'Shea and Maguire were standing on the path leading from the road to Westport House. A huge 4x4 with Armed Response Support stencilled on the side was there too, and three Gardaí dressed all in black with Heckler & Koch MP5s raised to their shoulders. Shane Nevin had been kitted out with a stab-proof vest and was leading the armed Gardaí up across the grass towards the copse where the man was encamped.

They crept along slowly, making almost no noise at all, till they were able to surround the tent. When the Gardaí were in position, they signalled for Shane to withdraw. One of the Gardaí advanced on the sleeping form in the tent and kicked his feet. The man stirred and found himself looking into the masked faces of the ARU officers, their guns aimed, the bright white weapon lights shining in his face.

It took another hour to get the man back to the Garda station. All his belongings had to be collected, and the motorbike had to be loaded onto a truck and driven back too. When he arrived at the Garda station, he was booked in and put in a cell.

Maguire spoke to him before he disappeared into his cell for the night. "You'll be detained here until the morning. We'll be interviewing you then, and you can have legal representation if you want. Oh, and we'll need to take a DNA sample too. Once we've done that, try to get some sleep."

The desk sergeant was given the task of collecting the DNA sample from the suspect. He used a swab stick on the inside of his mouth and carefully placed it in a glass tube, before labelling it and sending it out to the forensic laboratory.

Before Maguire left, she went to the back of the station where the Honda had now been unloaded and parked. She went to the back of the bike and opened the large black box affixed above the rear mudguard. It wasn't locked. Inside, she found a laptop, a large sheaf of papers that on first glance looked very technical and, beneath all of that, two bricks of €50 notes wrapped in plastic.

She smiled to herself as she took the haul back into the station, placed the lot into paper evidence bags, sealed them, wrote the details on the outside of the bags and placed them in the evidence locker.

Finally, they had their killer.

Chapter Thirty-Six

The following morning was grey and overcast in Westport. Some people said that there were two kinds of weather in the county – rain and heavy rain, but this was somewhat unjust, although the county did benefit from the persistent south-westerly winds that brought a lot of moisture from the Atlantic Ocean to the place.

But when Deirdre Maguire and Martin O'Shea got to the Garda station at just before 9 a.m., they were in good spirits. As part of the tidying-up operation in the small hours of the morning, they'd relieved Shane Nevin of the knife he'd been carrying, and that would go to the forensic laboratory for analysis. Shane had told them where he'd found it, and though they weren't sure whether it would be any good as evidence of his father's and brother's killing, they might not need it in any case, given the stack of evidence they had against their man.

Before they went downstairs to interview the suspect, Maguire asked Agnes Gallagher if she'd had any luck tracking down Fu Li Chung.

"No, sorry, boss. There are millions of them on Google. I tried sending a WhatsApp to the phone number, but it was never picked up."

"OK. Well, try getting on to the firm that supply the cheese company in China. I think it's called Chi-Supp. See if they can help you with this bloke, Chung."

"OK. I'll try. But my Chinese is a bit rusty," Gallagher said, smiling.

Maguire joined O'Shea in his office, but as the two detectives were preparing to interview their captor, the desk sergeant rang, advising that a solicitor had arrived at the front desk claiming to represent him.

"Cripes! We didn't send for her, did we?" Maguire when O'Shea had finished the call and brought her up to date.

"Definitely not. But now that she's here, we'd better see how the land lies."

The two of them made their way downstairs to greet the woman, who was waiting in the reception area of the station. She was tall, probably in her mid-forties and immaculately turned out in a mid-grey business suit, and carrying an expensive-looking leather briefcase.

O'Shea opened the conversation. "Good morning. I'm Detective Inspector Martin O'Shea, and this is my colleague, Detective Sergeant Deirdre Maguire," he said, extending his hand to be shaken.

"Good morning, Inspector. I'm Megan O'Reilly from O'Reilly, Hays and Byrne. I'm here to represent Barry Turner, whom I believe you arrested last night. I'd like to have some time with my client before you begin to interview him. May I ask what charge you've detained him under?"

O'Shea gave his sergeant a puzzled look. "Well, at least we now have a name for the man. May I ask who informed you that Mr Turner was in custody?" he asked the solicitor.

"That's none of your business, Inspector. May I assume that the correct procedure was carried out when you detained my client?"

"Absolutely. And there are several members of the Gardaí that can attest to that if required. Now, will thirty minutes be sufficient for you? And perhaps we could get you a cup of tea or coffee?"

"That won't be necessary. If you could just show me to an interview room and bring Mr Turner to me please, and yes, half an hour will suffice."

They left the desk sergeant to escort the solicitor to interview room one and retrieve Turner.

"What do you make of that, Deirdre?" O'Shea asked as they made their way back upstairs.

"A bit odd. How the hell did she know we had her precious Mr Turner here at all? But it's good to have a name for the bugger at least. I'll get Agnes digging to see what she can find on him."

"Good idea. We'll reconvene when her ladyship is ready for us."

* * *

When they were all present in the rather crowded interview room, Megan O'Reilly was the first to speak.

"Inspector, my client advises me that during his arrest last night, when he was camped peacefully in the grounds of the country estate, he was manhandled by your officers and sustained some injuries. May I ask if you've requested a medical examination of Mr Turner?"

"I can assure you, Ms O'Reilly, that your client did not sustain any injuries at our hands during his detention. I was there the whole time. If he has any injuries, then we had nothing to do with it, and neither did he mention anything about injuries last night during his arrest. However, if your client wishes to be medically examined, then it can be arranged, but we will, in any case, proceed with our interview, as he seems perfectly fit to answer our questions, whilst we await the attendance of a doctor."

O'Reilly looked at Turner, and O'Shea perceived a very slight, almost imperceptible, shake of their heads.

"Very well, Inspector. We'll leave the doctor for now. Why exactly have you arrested Mr Turner? It can't be trespass. As I understand it, the place where he was camped is common land."

O'Shea smiled. "It's not common land, Ms O'Reilly, but it isn't uncommon for people to camp out there. No, it's not trespass."

"So what is it then?"

"Well, let's see. There's quite a long list of crimes. Sergeant, would you like to tell Ms O'Reilly?" O'Shea asked.

"Yes, sir, of course. Let's start with theft," Maguire said, addressing the woman. "During a forensic examination of the motorcycle that was in your client's possession, we discovered two items which we believe to be stolen. I refer here to a sheaf of documents that we believe were the property of a Mr Conor Nevin, and a laptop belonging to the same individual. We'd like to know how Mr Turner came by these items."

"Is that all? My client denies any wrongdoing in relation to these items. He says he bought the laptop, and the documents were stored upon it, and he had them printed out when he acquired it."

"I see," Maguire said, "and I presume Mr Turner can provide us with a receipt for the purchase of the laptop? After all, it's a top-of-the-range model, so it was hardly cheap."

"Mr Turner didn't actually get a receipt for the item, and before you ask, he paid cash," O'Reilly said calmly.

"We'll come back to that in a moment. I should also say that we wish to question your client in connection with the murder of Conor Nevin and his father Pat, who were brutally killed at their home just over a week ago."

"What! That's outrageous! Why didn't you say so?" O'Reilly demanded, her demeanour now a little less calm.

"I was getting there, Ms O'Reilly. Now, what can your client tell us about the killing of the Nevins?"

"Absolutely nothing. He has no idea what you're talking about."

O'Shea decided to cut in. "And there's the matter of the theft of the laptop we found in your possession from one of our officers. That's very serious."

"That silly cow gave it to me. She just handed it over nice as pie," Turner said, to the obvious annoyance of his brief.

"So you admit to holding Agnes Gallagher's parents hostage and under threat at their home, while Agnes went and retrieved the laptop from our evidence locker then?"

O'Reilly interrupted. "Say nothing. Not a word."

"May I ask you, Mr Turner, what you're doing here in Westport?" O'Shea went on.

"I'm on holiday. I've been touring around on my bike. It's nice around here."

"It is indeed. But something puzzles me. I think if I had several thousand euro in cash in the back box of my motorbike, I might choose to spend a little of it by staying in a hotel or at least a bed and breakfast. Why camp out in the rain?"

"I like to be close to nature, don't I?" Turner said, managing to keep a straight face.

Maguire took over again. "Mr Turner, the motorbike you have in your possession – could you tell us where exactly you acquired it, and how?"

"I bought it in Birmingham. From a dealer. Cost me a right lot, it did, but it's a good 'un."

"I see," Maguire went on. "So presumably you have no idea why it has false registration plates then? The number it's displaying belongs to a Royal Mail delivery van."

Turner looked, a little plaintively, at his brief.

"Mr Turner has no idea, Sergeant. As he said, he purchased the bike from a dealer in Birmingham," O'Reilly said.

"And presumably Mr Turner has a receipt for such a significant purchase, or a guarantee, or something on paper at least?" Maguire asked.

"I lost it," Turner said.

"How very careless of you. Can you at least give us the name of the dealer where you bought the bike, Mr Turner?"

"I've forgotten. Some big place near King's Heath."

"Very well. We'll be adding various motoring offences to the ever-lengthening list of charges for you, Mr Turner. I suggest we take a break now. Shall we say 2:30? We have some things to follow up," O'Shea said.

Chapter Thirty-Seven

Back in the open-plan area, things were busy. As O'Shea and Maguire arrived back from interviewing Turner, Agnes Gallagher approached.

"Have you got a minute, boss?" she asked Maguire.

"Yes, of course. What have you got?"

"Quite a bit actually. Let's sit down, and I'll tell you all."

O'Shea went into his office, while Maguire accompanied the younger officer to her desk.

"OK. Well, firstly, we found a mobile phone in amongst Turner's stuff at the campsite. Now there's not a lot on it, just one number in fact. It's a Dutch prefix, and I've called it from an anonymous phone, but it appears to be out of service."

"Is there any call history on Turner's phone, or any texts or anything?" Maguire asked.

"No, nothing like that. He's been quite careful. But there's more, boss."

"Go on."

"Well, you know we found a stash of cash too. I had a careful look at the notes, and I can tell from the initial character of the serial numbers that they were all issued in the Netherlands. Each of the eurozone countries uses a different initial letter signifying where the notes were issued, and P is for the Netherlands."

"Did you check them all?"

"No, but I took several out from each block, and they're all the same."

"OK, Agnes, that's good work. Not much doubt we have a Dutch connection. Keep digging – see if you can find any other links to the Netherlands."

"No problem."

"Great. The DI and I have to go back down to talk to Mr Turner. This might help loosen his tongue. See you later, but if you get anything amazing, come and tell us, won't you?"

"Yes, of course."

Maguire then went into O'Shea's office and updated the inspector on what Gallagher had discovered.

"That's all very well, Deirdre, but does it get us any nearer to being able to charge him with the murders? We need more information," O'Shea said.

"Well, it looks as if Turner was paid handsomely to do the deadly deed, and it gives us another connection to the Netherlands."

O'Shea frowned. "The Netherlands?"

"The cheese woman said they got that inulin stuff from an outfit in Holland, remember? And Agnes has just told me that Turner's phone had a Dutch number on it."

O'Shea clicked his fingers. "Right. So we have contaminated inulin coming from the Netherlands; cash from the same place; a mysterious phone number with a Dutch dialling code; and an Englishman on a stolen motorbike going around killing people and assaulting one of our officers to get hold of Conor Nevin's research. Surely we can make something out of all of that?"

"Something, certainly, but not murder."

"Not yet anyway. Never mind. Let's go and get some lunch. Are you hungry?" O'Shea asked.

"Yes, I'm starving. Nelsons?"

"Yes. Let's go," O'Shea said, getting up and locking his PC screen before putting on his jacket.

* * *

Nelsons was a fashionable bistro-style eatery just a short walk from the Garda station on Westport High Street. It had been open for almost two years now and was popular with the townspeople, who enjoyed the freshly prepared dishes and the ambiance, along with a glass or two of good wine. At lunchtime on dreary wet days – of which there were many in Mayo – the place was very uncrowded, so O'Shea and Maguire had no trouble getting a table in the window, looking out onto the street.

When they were seated, O'Shea opened the conversation. "So tell me Deirdre, how are things in your world just now?"

"How do you mean, sir?"

"It's Martin when we're not on duty, remember? Just generally, you know?"

"All good, boss. I'm enjoying the work here, although I never thought we'd see a double murder in Westport. It's a fine state things have come to. We have a good team though, and I think we'll crack it. What about you?" Maguire asked, attempting to turn the spotlight away from herself.

"Oh, fine. You mentioned before you were seeing someone – how's that all going?" he asked, smiling a little.

"It's still casual."

"Have you been seeing him for long – assuming it is a he?"

Maguire gave her boss a withering look before replying. "Yes, Martin, it is a he. One X and one Y chromosome, and before you ask, I have two X chromosomes, and there's no doubt about either of us!"

"Sorry, that was a bit insensitive. What does he do for a living?"

"He's in insurance. It's not as boring as it sounds. He's an investigator for that big place out the far side of Castlebar. He looks into any big claims for theft or damage to make sure everything is above board before they pay out. You'd be surprised at the things he comes across."

"Is that how you met him?" O'Shea asked.

"Yes. There was a so-called theft of an allegedly valuable bit of yellow plant from a builder's yard. The owner put in a claim for €60,000, which raised a few eyebrows at the insurance company. Eoin investigated, and it turned out the builder was on hard times and had driven the bulldozer into a lake himself. It was only worth about €5,000. I had to charge the bloke when it all came to light, and that's when I met Eoin."

"Cool. Do you see things becoming more serious between you?"

Just like when they'd gone for a drink, Maguire was beginning to feel a little uncomfortable with the personal nature of the questions her colleague was asking. "Like I said, we'll see. What about you? Your wife is a nurse, isn't she?"

"Yes. She works at the hospital in Castlebar. It's quite a tough job, but she enjoys it. She's a very caring person."

"Does she worry about your job? You know, the risk aspect of it?"

"I'm sure she does, but she doesn't say anything. She knows I love it, and anyway, I haven't been stabbed or shot at for ages now, so it's all good!"

Maguire laughed as the waitress arrived with their food.

Chapter Thirty-Eight

"Well, Mr Turner, you've had some time to think about your situation. Is there anything you'd like to tell us?" O'Shea asked as he and Maguire resumed their interrogation of the man.

Turner looked to his lawyer for inspiration, and she shook her head almost imperceptibly. The detectives recognized the drill.

"No, nothing, except that you need to let me out of here. I ain't done nothing."

"Now, that's not really the case, is it? But to be honest, I'm not too bothered about your antics with Conor's laptop, or the fact that you seem to have a whole pile of cash that I very much doubt you earned honestly," O'Shea said. "I'm much more concerned about the killing of Pat and Conor Nevin. Now, if you could just tell us what all that was about, we might be getting somewhere."

"No comment."

Everyone remained silent for quite a few moments. O'Shea and Maguire were looking expectantly at their suspect, but he just stared at the floor.

"Tell us about the Dutch connection, Mr Turner," Maguire said.

Turner visibly flinched but recovered quickly. "I don't know what you're talking about."

"But I think you do," Maguire said. "After all, we found a Netherlands phone number on your mobile, and all that lovely money you had in the back of your bike came from Holland too. So I think you know very well what I'm talking about. Who's your contact in the Netherlands?"

"No comment."

Megan O'Reilly intervened. "Really, Sergeant, this is very fanciful. My client is British. He's here on holiday, and he has somehow inadvertently got caught up in some horrible crime that he knows nothing about. Now, as you know, you can only detain him for 24 hours and your time will be up soon enough. So are you going to charge my client, or can we leave?"

"I most certainly *am* going to charge your client, Ms O'Reilly," Maguire replied. "We've already discussed a number of serious charges that we intend to bring against him. I just thought I'd give Mr Turner an opportunity to tell us about the other crimes he's been involved in. After all, if we had the full picture, we might be able to do something about the less serious charges."

O'Shea gave his partner a slightly quizzical look.

Before O'Reilly had time to reply, there was a knock on the door.

Maguire went and opened it. It was Agnes Gallagher.

"Sorry, boss, but I think you need to see this," Gallagher said, handing Maguire a Manilla folder.

"What am I looking at?"

"It's from forensics. They've found evidence of Turner handling the knife, and some traces of Pat Nevin's blood.

Conor's too. It's not a whole lot, but they say it should be enough to get us into court, in any case."

Maguire smiled. "Thanks, Agnes. Nice timing too."

She closed the door and resumed her seat, placing the Manilla folder down on the table in front of her.

"Mr Turner, my colleague has just delivered a report from our forensic laboratory. You may be aware that we took a knife from Shane Nevin, Pat Nevin's other son and Conor Nevin's brother. He found it in the stream close to the scene of the crime. He was contemplating using it on you as you slept in your sleeping bag, but fortunately for you, he's a decent lad and thought better of it – though frankly I wouldn't have blamed him if he *had* gone through with it."

"And what exactly has this to do with my client, Sergeant?"

"What exactly this has to do with your client, Ms O'Reilly, is that we recovered DNA samples from the knife. Skin flakes found caught in the handle of the knife match Mr Turner's DNA, and small blood particles that had lodged near the hilt of the weapon are from the Nevins. What would you like to say to that, Mr Turner?" Maguire asked.

Turner had turned a funny shade of grey. He looked to O'Reilly, as if somehow she could get him out of the hole he was in, but the solicitor just looked stony-faced. After a tense few minutes, Turner buried his head in his hands and muttered, "All right, all right! Fair cop."

Megan O'Reilly reached out and placed her hand on Turner's forearm. "I would advise you to say nothing more, Mr Turner. Nothing at all."

"Ah, what's the use? It sounds as if this lot have me

bang to rights. Yes, yes, I killed the two Nevins," he said to the detectives. "So what? They was about to blow the whole caper wide open. Hundreds of people would have lost their jobs, and millions would have gone up in smoke. But maybe we could help each other still? What do you say?"

* * *

Barry Turner took a small scruffy piece of paper out of his jeans pocket and unfolded it. Then he picked up the mobile phone that Maguire had given him, and keyed in the number on the sliver of paper slowly and deliberately. Before pressing the green button to activate the call, he looked up at O'Shea and Maguire. "I hope this works. He's no eejit, you know."

"I'm sure it'll be fine, Barry. Now just get on and make the call."

Turner did as he was told, placing the little phone on loudspeaker mode.

After two rings, a male voice came on the line. "*Ja*," the man said.

"Hello, Hendrik, it's me," Turner said.

"I told you not to call me. What do you want?"

"I need some more money. Things are getting very tricky here. The cops nabbed my bike, and the cash you left for me was in the back box. So I can't get out of here. I'm skint. And I need to leave the country sharpish. I think they're on to me."

"Bloody hell! What do you expect me to do about it? No, Barry. You're on your own this time."

"Now hold on. That's not very smart. After all, if I get nabbed, I might be tempted to tell the cops everything I know, and that would be, shall we say, a little inconvenient for you."

Blaat thought for a moment. "Tell you what. Why don't I come and get you? I can drop you off in the UK on my way back. And I'll bring some extra cash too. But not a word. And stay out of sight till you hear from me. OK?"

"Yeah, OK. No tricks now. You can call me on this number."

The line went dead.

"How did I do?" Turner asked.

"Fair, Barry. Not brilliantly but fair. How will this fella get here?" O'Shea asked.

"He'll get the ferry to Harwich or somewhere like that, then drive to Holyhead and come across to Dublin. He won't want to risk a flight, and he'll probably be armed too."

"Right. We'll be ready for him."

Chapter Thirty-Nine

"So tell us, Barry: how did you get hold of the money we found stashed in your motorbike?" Maguire asked.

Turner was back in the interview room.

"That was easy. It was put in a left luggage locker in Westport railway station."

"And how did you get the key?"

"It was taped to the back of the no parking sign outside the station. Blaat left it there when he dropped the cash."

"Tell us more about why the Nevins had to be silenced. You mentioned jobs and money would've been lost. Is that true? There might have been a bit of a scandal about the inulin locally, but it would have blown over, wouldn't it? These kinds of things happen all the time, and there's usually no long-term damage," Maguire said.

"The Chinese are scared shitless about any reputational impact on their sales. They sell millions – maybe billions – of dollars' worth of supplements into Europe, and anything that might disrupt that business could be very awkward," Turner said.

O'Shea and Maguire digested what Turner had said, then Maguire asked Turner, "Did you ever hear of a man called Fu Li Chung?"

"No, can't say that I have. Who's he then?"

"It doesn't matter. Have you had any dealings with the Chinese?"

"Not bleeding likely. Some of them can be vicious bastards."

"Right, well you stay here till you hear from Blaat. Then let us know the arrangements, and we'll take it from there. OK?"

"Yeah, right. What will happen to me then?"

"Not for us to say. But your help with this will be taken into account, don't worry."

* * *

Superintendent Derry O'Connell wasn't happy.

"Are you sure about this, Martin? It all seems a bit hare-brained to me. And if it goes wrong, there'll be a hell of a fuss."

O'Shea shuffled uncomfortably in his seat. "Look, one way or the other, we have Turner for the double murder of Pat and Conor Nevin. That's solid. We have forensics and the man's own words to back it up. He'll be going down for a nice long time, don't worry. As for the Dutchman, we should get him on conspiracy to murder as well, and Turner says he'll probably be armed when he gets here. He'll want to take care of Turner himself to close down the whole thing."

"Yes, but you have to see this from my perspective. We can't afford to have any connection between the cheese company and the death of the Nevins. Their reputation – and the reputation of the entire west of Ireland – would be thrashed. It would give a whole new meaning to the Wild Atlantic Way," O'Connell said.

"OK. I hear you, sir. Let me see if I can get the press office to concoct some kind of yarn. Maybe a case of mistaken identity to do with some gang activity in the area or something."

"Will the Nevins go along with it?"

"I'll have a word. The other brother, Shane, is a good lad. Once we tell him that Turner's going down for the murders, and that his brother's research has helped to close down an international food scam, he should be happy enough. He has more things to be worrying him now anyway, as he's the sole breadwinner out at the farm."

"What about the cheese woman?"

"She won't want too much fuss. She can recall whatever product she has out in the shops on some pretext and find another supplier of inulin, or maybe she'll just not bother using the additive any more. I might suggest that to her."

"Are you sure you can keep a lid on it all?" O'Connell asked. "What about Maguire?"

"Don't worry on that score, sir. She's making arrangements to hand the Dutchman over to the boys in Dublin if we're successful in nabbing him. She's happy to pass on the glory in this instance, but she's been excellent all along."

"Hmph. OK. Off you go then. But for God's sake, Martin, don't let this blow up in our faces."

"Don't worry, sir – it'll be fine."

* * *

"Any luck with your Chinese friend, Agnes?" Maguire asked.

"No, boss. I did manage to speak to the company, but they say they don't have a Fu Li Chung working for them.

So that's a bit of a dead end."

"Shit! OK, well, leave it then. Did we ever get anywhere with Conor Nevin's nemesis – what was his name, McGinty or something?"

"Oh, yes. Liam followed up on that. I think he wrote it up in the file. McGinty's apparently transferred to Letterkenny to finish his degree. He wasn't around when the Nevins were killed."

"OK. Thanks, Agnes. I haven't had time to read the file for the last few days, but that's another loose end tied up."

Maguire went in search of O'Shea, who was sitting pensively in his office staring out the window.

"Sorry, boss. But how do you want to play this thing with our motorbiking friend downstairs?"

"Hi, Deirdre. I was just putting that together in my head. Presumably, Turner will get a message from Blaat about his arrival into the country. We can intercept him then, and with a bit of luck, he'll have a weapon on him, and we can get him on that. Once we have that sewn up, we'll see what else we can do. With the both of them in custody, that should send a clear message back to the Chinese not to mess with us. What do you think?"

"Hmm… quite a lot of ifs and maybes in that plan, boss. Have you got a plan B?"

"Eh, no, not really. We'll have to improvise if plan A doesn't work. But it should be OK," he said, not sounding too confident.

"Whatever you say, boss," she said, echoing the sentiment.

Chapter Forty

It was just before lunchtime as the Stena Line ferry berthed at the pier in Dublin port. The weather was cool, and the breeze off the sea made it feel even colder. Turner had received a text message from Blaat announcing his arrival and suggesting they meet at 8 p.m. in the grounds of Westport House.

O'Shea and Maguire had teamed up with a squad of four officers from Dublin's Store Street Garda station, and they were all dressed in plain clothes, standing around in the area where vehicles would disembark from the huge ship.

When the bow doors opened and the ramp had been lowered, lorries started to emerge from the vessel in a seemingly endless stream. When the first deck of trucks had been emptied, a ramp inside the ship was lowered, and cars, which had been stowed on the upper deck, made their way slowly to the exit.

Maguire had been in touch with the ferry company the previous afternoon and taken down the registration number, make and model of Blaat's car, and circulated it to the team. After 15 or so cars had reached terra firma, they saw the black Volvo S60 which was their target, leaving the ferry. Two of the Store Street Gardaí stepped out into the line and indicated the Volvo to pull over. It came to rest behind a parked lorry, and the Garda went to the driver's door, gestured for the Dutchman to wind down the window and said, "Mr Blaat, could you please switch off the engine and exit the car?"

As the Dutchman emerged from his vehicle, the other Gardaí closed in around him so that he couldn't make a run for it. This didn't stop him protesting loudly however.

"What's going on? I'm just a tourist. Why are you detaining me?"

O'Shea faced the man. "Mr Blaat, we have reason to believe that there may be a firearm in your vehicle. As I'm sure you're aware, importing a firearm into Ireland is completely against the law, so please just wait here with me while my officers examine your car."

* * *

Meanwhile, Maguire had spoken to two of the uniformed officers who were starting to search Blaat's car, looking in the footwells, the glove compartment, the boot and underneath the seats.

After a few minutes, one of them approached Maguire. "There's nothing in it, Sarge; it's clean."

Maguire nodded at the man and walked over to the car; all of its doors stood open.

"Hang on a minute. Look here," she said, pointing to the rear passenger's door on the left-hand side of the vehicle. "The door card isn't properly secured."

The Garda she'd been speaking to got down on his hunkers and gently prised the door card away from the frame with his fingers. Loud pops could be heard as the fasteners holding it in place gave way. As the last one released its grip, the door card rotated by 90 degrees, so it was now just held on by the door handle. Behind it, a cavity between the inner door frame and the outer skin was revealed, and there, wrapped in a cloth and a plastic bag, was an item that looked like a gun.

Maguire donned blue vinyl gloves and carefully removed the package. She opened the plastic bag, handing it to the nearest officer, and unwrapped the contents – a Glock 9 mm handgun that appeared to have a full clip of bullets.

"Over here, boss," she called to O'Shea.

He came across and examined the weapon without touching it. "Good work, Deirdre. I'll read yer man his rights."

* * *

It took them most of the rest of the day to get back to Westport. Blaat had been handcuffed and was traveling in the back of O'Shea's car, seated beside Maguire. He remained totally silent for the entire journey.

When they got back to the Garda station, Blaat was booked in and advised that he could have a solicitor to represent him, but that they wouldn't start questioning him until the following day. In the meantime, he was to remain in a cell where he would be provided with food and water, and made as comfortable as possible for the night.

Before they left the Garda station for the night, O'Shea and Maguire agreed to have a think about how best to handle to the two men. O'Shea was sure they could get Turner to tell them everything he knew – they just had to give him the right incentive.

Chapter Forty-One

Before the interviews started the following morning, O'Shea and Maguire got together over a cup of coffee.

"So how do you want to play this, boss?" Maguire asked.

"It's tricky, 'cos Turner has committed two murders after all, so we can't really promise him anything. I mean, assuming the evidence we have stands up, he'll be going down for 15 years at least, and in any case, I wouldn't want to see anything less for him."

"Yes, I know. But I've been thinking about it overnight. We could tell him that if he cooperates, it could be mentioned at his trial, and the judge could take it into account. And we might be able to do something about the cash we found on him too."

"What do you mean?"

"Well, it's only us that knows how much he had stashed in the bike. What if some of that was his personal money and not connected to the crimes? It could make things a bit more comfortable for him in prison."

"Cripes, Deirdre, that's all a bit dodgy, don't you think? His brief would be on to that like a fly on a cowpat. Anyway, let's start with him. We can leave the Dutchman till after."

* * *

"Good morning, Mr Turner. I hope you had a comfortable night. Now, let's get started, shall we?" Maguire said as she and O'Shea took their seats. Megan O'Reilly was there too, looking very professional in her mid-grey business suit and white blouse. She took out a yellow legal pad and her fancy Mont Blanc pen, ready for action.

O'Shea opened the discussion. "Mr Turner, as you said yourself, we have you bang to rights for these two killings. But you have no idea how tragic this case is. Pat Nevin was a hard-working family man with two sons, and between them all, they ran a successful cattle farm and had good prospects. Pat ensured that his boys were getting the best possible education, so that they might have a better life – a life which you, in the case of Conor Nevin, brutally cut short. His wife and remaining son will never get over this."

"My heart bleeds, I'm sure," Turner said, looking at the floor.

O'Reilly looked a bit put out by her client's callousness and gave him a stern stare.

"But that's not the whole story, is it, Barry? What we need you to tell us is what exactly has been going on with Henrik Blaat," O'Shea said.

"What's in it for me?"

Maguire sat forward and put on a sympathetic expression. "Look, Barry, we want to help you. Now, it's obvious you're going to have to face the consequences of your actions, and that will almost certainly lead to a long custodial sentence. And as I'm sure you are aware, Englishmen don't always do too well in Irish prisons. But if you were to assist us with this other business – and given the fact you helped us apprehend Blaat in the first place – we might be able to make things a little easier for you. What do you say?"

O'Reilly was quick to respond. "What exactly are you suggesting, Sergeant?"

"Well, firstly, if you cooperate, we'll tell the judge at your trial that you've been helpful, and that could encourage him to suspend some of your sentence. And we could look again at the cash we found on you when you were arrested. Perhaps we were a little hasty there. It might not all be blood money."

"All sounds rather tenuous, Sergeant. Have you nothing more definitive to offer my client?" O'Reilly asked.

"Let's see what he can tell us, shall we, and then we'll be able to be more definitive, as you call it."

A tense silence filled the air. The detectives knew from experience to say no more at this stage. If Turner was going to spill the beans, he needed some time to process the matter.

After several minutes, he looked up at O'Shea. "Blaat isn't who you think he is. Oh, yes, he puts on a charade of being an up-and-coming executive in that place in Holland, but he's a crook. I've known him for years, and I can tell you, some of the stunts he's got up to would make you flinch. Blaat isn't his real name either. He used to be Edward de Groot, until that became, shall we say, inconvenient."

"I see. And how do you know him?" Maguire asked.

"We was involved in a caper way back robbing duty-free spirits from one of the ferry companies. Oh, don't worry, we got caught, but weasel de Groot managed to get out of it by blaming me, and I did three years in the clink for it."

"So why did you have anything to do with him on this occasion?" O'Shea asked.

"Money. I'm broke. I needed the cash, and it looked like a doddle. He called me in England and came over. We met in a pub, and he explained what he wanted. Seemed a handy one to me, and he said he would pay me well. So I took the gig."

"And you said you got the money from a left luggage locker, yes?" Maguire asked.

"Yeah, though I imagine he was going to take it back once he'd seen me off. You lot probably saved my life," Turner said.

"Well then, I think a little reciprocal gratitude might be in order," O'Shea said. "Are you prepared to give us a full statement with everything you know about Blaat, or de Groot, and the full lowdown on the crimes that have been committed over here, including the business with Agnes Gallagher, and the damage that was caused out at ATU?"

"I need a few minutes to confer with my client, Inspector. Could we take a fifteen-minute break?"

"Yes, of course, Ms O'Reilly. No problem. Would you like some refreshments?" O'Shea asked.

"Yes, please. Coffee would be lovely."

Once they were outside the interview room, O'Shea spoke to his colleague. "I'll organize the drinks. Can you go upstairs and get Agnes to contact the Dutch police? Give them the names Edward de Groot and Henrik Blaat, and see if they show any interest. Things are going OK with Turner. I reckon he'll go for a deal when Little Miss Prim and Proper has had a good chat with him."

"Yes, OK, boss. See you back here in fifteen minutes."

Chapter Forty-Two

Maguire found Agnes Gallagher at her desk.

"Agnes, the boss wants you to get on to the Dutch police and see if they have anything on Henrik Blaat, who may also be known to them as Edward de Groot. Apparently, yer man downstairs has form, and we need to have the details before we interview him. You can get a photo of him from the front desk if that helps."

"OK, Sarge. How's it going anyway?"

"Hmm… so-so. We're going in again in a few minutes. Let me know if you get anything useful from The Netherlands."

"Will do."

"Oh, and, Agnes, how much exactly was there in Turner's stash of €50 notes?"

"Liam and myself counted it out before we put it in the evidence room. There was €20,000 in it."

"Nice. Thanks."

Maguire went back downstairs to join O'Shea, and the two of them went back into the interview room.

"Well, Mr Turner, what's it to be?" O'Shea asked.

O'Reilly jumped in before her client could open his mouth. "What exactly are you offering my client, Inspector?"

"I'm making no promises, Ms O'Reilly, but with full cooperation from Mr Turner – and I mean full – we might be able to reduce the charges for the Nevins' killings to manslaughter. That would mean your client would get a much lighter sentence. After all, his intention was to rob Conor Nevin, was it not?"

"Is that all?" the woman pressed, sensing that she had the advantage.

"I've been thinking about the money too. If Mr Turner would agree to donate most of it to the college where he wrecked the computer laboratory, we might be able to let him keep the remainder. It would make it much easier for him while he served his sentence."

"What sort of spilt do you envisage?" O'Reilly asked.

"What about 15K to the college and 5K for your client?"

O'Reilly looked at Turner, who frankly couldn't believe his luck.

As if he was worried about getting carried away, O'Shea added, "But you'll have to testify against Blaat in court. We want him for conspiracy, which should get him a good few years here as a guest of the state."

Turner thought for a moment and rubbed his face with his hands. He didn't look quite so delighted when the implications of what had been said sank in.

"How long do you think I'll get inside?"

"It's not up to us, but if I was guessing, I'd say eight years with the last two or so suspended," O'Shea replied.

"OK. Deal."

"Not so fast, Mr Turner. This isn't a done deal. Not all of it is up to us. It's just our considered opinion of what may lie ahead for you."

"Yeah, OK. But you've done this before, right?"

"Yes. Many times," O'Shea said then turned to Maguire.

"Sergeant, can you look after Mr Turner from here? I want to go and talk to our other guest."

"Yes, of course, boss."

* * *

Before interviewing Blaat, O'Shea went back upstairs to speak to Agnes Gallagher.

"Hi, Agnes. Anything back from the Dutch police?"

"Yes, boss. I spoke to a really nice guy called de Kuyper. It took me a while to get through, but it was worth it. He told me they were indeed looking for de Groot. They didn't know he'd changed his name. They thought he'd gone abroad. They have a total of three warrants out for him, and de Kuyper asked me if they could issue a European arrest warrant for him and have him back. He's going to call back later. He needs to speak to his boss."

"Hmm… we'll see about that. But that is interesting. Thanks."

With this new information, O'Shea decided he needed to speak to the superintendent before he spoke to Blaat, or de Groot or whatever his name was. He made his way upstairs to O'Connell's office.

"Come," boomed the voice of the senior man when O'Shea knocked on his door.

"Ah, good morning, Martin. I was hoping you might pop in. I need an update on the Nevin case. There're a few people up in Dublin getting restless, not to mention the press office."

O'Shea brought his boss up to date with everything they knew so far and asked, "What do you reckon, sir?"

"Give me a minute. Let's just be clear. We have this Turner fella all tied up for the killings – is that right?"

"Yes. He's admitted it, and there's enough forensic evidence now to convict him even if he changes his mind. I doubt if he will though. He has hopes of pleading manslaughter. And he's been helpful to us in dealing with the Dutchman."

"And what exactly have we got on this bloke from the Netherlands?"

"We caught him bringing in a loaded Glock 9 mm handgun into the country, and Turner has told us that it was he who commissioned the murders. Apparently, there's millions of euro tied up in this business with the contaminated inulin, and the Chinese or whoever can't afford to let the word get out," O'Shea replied.

"Dutch, Chinese – God be with the days when all we had to deal with around here was a few lads hammering the shit out of each other after a night in the pub. I don't know. What do you want to do with this Blaat character?" O'Connell asked.

"Well, obviously, we could charge him with firearms offences, and maybe conspiracy to murder. But that's a bit tenuous. It relies on Turner's testimony, and a good brief could probably cast doubts on the veracity of evidence from a fellow villain and co-conspirator as it were."

"I see what you mean. Have you spoken to the Dutch police?"

"Not personally, sir. Agnes Gallagher has been in touch with them, and they're quite keen to have Mr de Groot back in their care," O'Shea said.

"OK, well how about this. You have a chat with our European colleagues. See what they have on yer man. If it's serious, as in he would be locked up for a good long spell in Holland, then let's hand him over. We don't want him getting off here on a technicality and walking free. God knows what he'd get up to. Does that sound OK to you?"

"Yes, sir. I'll go and call them now, and I'll let you know."

"Thanks. And don't go too soft on the other fella. We can't have British thugs running around the country causing mayhem."

"Yes, I agree, sir."

Chapter Forty-Three

Back downstairs, O'Shea asked Agnes Gallagher for the phone number for de Kuyper then took the Post-it note into his office and called the number. The phone rang three times and was answered by a man with a distinct Dutch accent.

"De Kuyper," he said.

"Hello, Mr de Kuyper. My name is Detective Inspector Martin O'Shea from the Irish police. I think you've been talking to a colleague of mine – DC Agnes Gallagher."

"Oh, yes. This is about Edward de Groot, yes?" De Kuyper said.

"Yes, that's right. I just wanted to ask you what sort of charges you'd be bringing against him if he went back to the Netherlands?"

"Ah, yes. Well, let me see. He's wanted for a serious assault on a man and his wife in their home. Some very nice jewellery was stolen and a good amount of cash, and the man in particular was very badly injured. He's also wanted as a suspect in a smuggling ring that were bringing in bootleg vodka and gin from the Far East. But then he virtually vanished, and I understand he's now calling himself Blaat – is that right?"

"Yes, that's what we believe. But, if, for example, we were to hand him over to you, would he be detained in prison, or would he be bailed?" O'Shea asked.

"He would definitely be detained, probably for some years. And if we can get him for the smuggling too, then that period of time would be extended. Why do you ask?"

"My superior officer, Detective Superintendent O'Connell, believes it might be best if we sent him back to you. We only have him on bringing a firearm into Ireland. There's more for us to investigate, but it's very complex, and I'm not sure if we would get to hold him until we figure it all out."

"I see. Well, it would be a feather in our caps if we had him back here and we could lock him up. How would you like to proceed, Inspector?"

"Give me a day or so. I'll let you know what the position is. Would you be able to send someone to collect him, or would we need to deliver him to you?" O'Shea asked.

"Oh, no, we would be happy to come and get him. Yes, please let me know what you've decided, and thank you, Inspector."

"I will. Thanks. Bye for now."

When he'd finished the call, O'Shea asked Maguire to come into his office. He told her about his chat upstairs, and the call he'd had with the Dutch police.

"Yes, and while you were doing all that, I spoke to the DPP about Turner. They won't go for manslaughter. The want a charge of murder and to let the judge decide how long he'll have to serve."

"Looks like it's not his lucky day then. Do you want to tell him, or shall I?"

"Why don't myself and Agnes give him the good news? It'll make her feel better after what he did to her and her family."

"Excellent. Then I can make the arrangements with the Dutch for the other fella."

* * *

Maguire collected Agnes Gallagher.

"The boss wants us to get Turner back in and tell him that he's going down for double murder. The DPP won't hear of a plea deal for manslaughter, and in any case, it looks as if Blaat is heading back to the Netherlands," Maguire said.

"Cripes! I'm going to enjoy this, boss. Let's go!"

Turner was brought back into the interview room. When he was seated opposite Maguire and Gallagher, he said, "Do I need my solicitor back?"

"No, Mr Turner. We aren't here to question you," Maguire said and looked to her colleague.

Gallagher got the message and looked directly into Turner's eyes. "Mr Turner, we're going to charge you with the murder of Patrick and Conor Nevin, and the assault on myself, as well as various driving offences. Have you anything to say?"

"I thought we had a deal?" Turner replied, the colour draining from his face.

"No, Mr Turner, we didn't. And for your information, there will be no need for you to testify against Henrik Blaat, or whatever his name really is," Maguire said.

"But you said I would be able to plead manslaughter. This is shite!"

"Tell it to someone who cares. Now, if you'd like to come with me, I'll take you outside to the desk sergeant and he'll record the charge. You'll be brought to court as soon as it can be arranged," Gallagher said.

Epilogue

Turner was brought to court the following morning and was charged with the murders of Pat Nevin and his son, Conor. The Gardaí advised the court that other charges were likely to follow, and as they deemed Turner to be a flight risk, bail was denied.

Later, when the case came to trial, which lasted two weeks, the jury took just 80 minutes to find him guilty, and he was sentenced to life in prison. Although the judges in Ireland couldn't, as yet, set a minimum tariff, they could recommend a minimum term, and in this case, Judge Buckley suggested that twenty years might be appropriate. The motorcycle Turner had been riding was eventually traced back to its original owner in Manchester, and the man came to Ireland to claim it and ride it back to the United Kingdom, complete with its original registration number on plates he'd brought with him. The money that Turner had been paid was seized by the state.

The Dutch police tried to pursue the Chinese connection but weren't successful in their efforts. However, they did manage to stop the importation of the contaminated inulin into the entire EU.

Shane Nevin decided not to pass his father's cattle on to the neighbour. Working virtually around the clock, what with his schoolwork as well as tending to the farm, he kept the animals on the land until they were ready for slaughter.

"It's what Dad would have wanted," he said to his mother, who was slowly coming to terms with her loss. When the case was over, Shane received Conor's laptop back from the Gardaí and used it to help run the farm.

Mrs Blenerhassett recalled as much of the contaminated cheese as she could, telling her customers that there was some chance an impurity had found its way into the product. She stopped using any bulking agent at all after that, and the flavour of the cheese improved considerably.

Henrik Blaat, also known as Edward de Groot, was collected by the Dutch police at Dublin airport and taken back to Amsterdam. He was arraigned on a variety of charges. His assets were confiscated and used to pay recompense to his victims, and he was given a sentence of 12 years.

Maeve Kilcoyne got to know Shane Nevin quite well after she'd got over the loss of Conor. She was often to be found helping out at the Nevins' farm at the weekends, and she was a great consolation to Mrs Nevin, who felt that with Maeve's presence, she still had a connection of sorts with her eldest son.

Derry O'Connell was pleased with the outcome of the case. Aided by a very willing press officer, much was made of the success by the Westport Gardaí in solving this perplexing case. O'Connell hosted a night out for all the Gardaí that had been involved, and thanked O'Shea and Maguire specifically for their efforts. Agnes Gallagher and Liam Staunton also got a mention in his praises.

But the warm glow of success in the Gardaí never lasts long. O'Shea and the team would soon be thrust into another dramatic case. But that's another story, for another day.

List of characters

Detective Inspector Martin O'Shea – a savvy senior police officer keen to make an impression in the newly organized Westport detective unit.

Detective Sergeant Deirdre Maguire – O'Shea's number two, who has a good nose for a wrong 'un.

Detective Garda Agnes Gallagher – a junior detective who lives at home with her parents

Detective Garda Liam Staunton – another young officer who shows promise

Superintendent Derry O'Connell – a senior detective who's keen to stamp his style on the new division

Pat Nevin – a hard-working cattle farmer who would do anything for his two sons

Conor Nevin – Pat's eldest son, who's studying agricultural science

Shane Nevin – Conor's younger brother, who's made of stern stuff

Eileen Nevin – Pat Nevin's wife

Bridget Mulligan – Eileen Nevin's sister

Eoin McNally – Deirdre Maguire's friend

Maeve Kilcoyne – Conor Nevin's girlfriend

Adam Wallace – Conor's mate from university

James McGinty – a would-be suitor of Maeve Kilcoyne

Professor Mulligan – Head of IT at Westport ATU

Ellis Williams – the rather dour administrator at Westport ATU

Dr Mulhall – the state pathologist

Kevin Walsh – a forensic officer

Barry Turner – a nasty criminal from the UK who likes motorcycling

Henrik Blaat – a Dutchman with a very iffy past

Mrs Blenerhassett – owns a craft cheese factory in Westport

Tom Dolan – Garda

Breda and Jimmy – paramedics

Sergeant O'Rahilly – the night man on duty in the Garda station
Mr Webster – secretary of the golf club

Mary Claffey – a student and computer operator at ATU

Aisling Crotty – a family liaison officer

Inspector de Kuyper – a Dutch police inspector

Printed by Amazon Italia Logistica S.r.l.
Torrazza Piemonte (TO), Italy

61134852R00122